CLIVE CUSSLER

The Adventures of
VIN FIZ

With illustrations by BILL FARNSWORTH

Philomel Books

PHILOMEL BOOKS

A division of Penguin Young Readers Group.

Published by The Penguin Group.

Penguin Group (USA) Inc., 375 Hudson Street, New York, NY 10014, U.S.A.

Penguin Group (Canada), 90 Eglinton Avenue East, Suite 700, Toronto, Ontario, Canada M4P 2Y3
(a division of Pearson Penguin Canada Inc.). Penguin Books Ltd, 80 Strand, London WC2R 0RL,
England. Penguin Ireland, 25 St. Stephen's Green, Dublin 2, Ireland (a division of Penguin Books Ltd.).
Penguin Group (Australia), 250 Camberwell Road, Camberwell, Victoria 3124, Australia
(a division of Pearson Australia Group Pty Ltd). Penguin Books India Pvt Ltd, 11 Community Centre,
Panchsheel Park, New Delhi -110 017, India. Penguin Group (NZ), Cnr Airborne and Rosedale Roads,
Albany, Auckland 1310, New Zealand (a division of Pearson New Zealand Ltd). Penguin Books
(South Africa) (Pty) Ltd, 24 Sturdee Avenue, Rosebank, Johannesburg 2196, South Africa.

Penguin Books Ltd, Registered Offices: 80 Strand, London WC2R 0RL, England.

Published simultaneously in Canada. Printed in the United States of America.

Design by Gunta Alexander. Text set in Wilke.

The cover illustration was rendered in oil paint on canvas, interiors in pencil.

Library of Congress Cataloging-in-Publication Data

Cussler, Clive. The adventures of Vin Fiz / Clive Cussler ; with illustrations by William Farnsworth.
p. cm. Summary: Ten-year-old twins Casey and Lacey fly an enchanted, antique airplane, named
the "Vin Fiz," across the United States and have several daring adventures along the way. Includes
historical notes on the real "Vin Fiz," the name of the airplane that made the first transcontinental
flight in 1911. [1. Airplanes—Fiction. 2. Voyages and travels—Fiction. 3. Rescues—Fiction.
4. Twins—Fiction. 5. Brothers and sisters—Fiction. 6. Magic—Fiction.] I. Farnsworth, William, ill.
II. Title. PZ7.C965 Ad 2006 [Fic]—dc22 2005048886 ISBN 0-399-24474-3

1 3 5 7 9 10 8 6 4 2

First Impression

For
Bryce & Lauren
&
Jason & Amie
&
Teri & Dirk & Dayna,
who heard it first

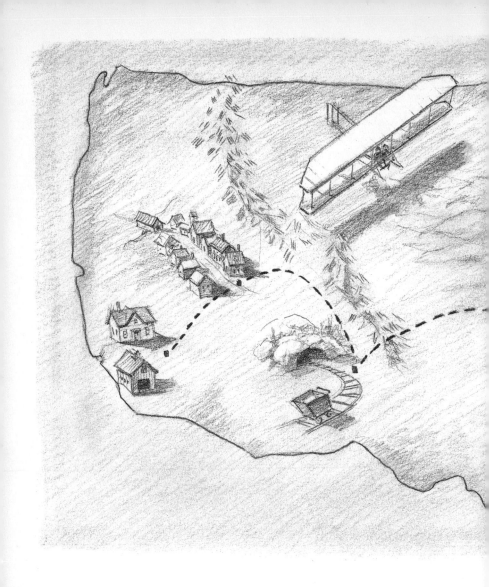

Casey and Lacey's Cross-Country Adventures

Contents

"I have a way with animals," said the stranger softly.

1

The Mysterious Stranger

In a time still remembered, there was a quaint little village in California called Castroville. It rested in a valley near the Pacific Ocean and was built on artichokes. Actually, they were not used to build the houses. Artichokes are too soft and do not make good building blocks. They are an edible flower head that is cooked and eaten as a vegetable. Some people like them, some do not. Some call artichokes an idiosyncrasy—a funny word that means odd behavior—because they really are a thistle with stickers whose leaves taste good only when dipped in a yummy sauce.

Every farm and family in the valley harvested artichokes . . . almost every farm and family, but not all. There was one man who did not follow the beat of an artichoke drummer. Ever Nicefolk preferred to grow exotic herbs and spices, valued for their savory taste and wonderful smells, and sell them to gourmet stores and restaurants around the country. On his little sixty-acre farm, he planted and raised licorice, spearmint, mint, figwort, ginseng and many other varieties during the growing season. The only problem was that he did not have enough land to be profitable. One bad year without rain and the Nicefolks would lose their farm.

Ever Nicefolk may sound like a curious name, but he could trace his family tree back five hundred years to an ancestor known as Knot Nicefolk, who was a highwayman in merry old England. A highwayman, you might like to know, was a bandit who held up travelers and stagecoaches. You've heard of Robin Hood, I'll bet—he was a highwayman too. Mr. Nicefolk was a serious man who seldom laughed but had twinkling gray eyes and wore a crooked smile that moved back and forth across his mouth as if unable to settle in one position. He moved and talked slowly, traits that fooled some into thinking he was dull witted, when in fact he was very clever and smart. A good man, an honest man, he was known throughout Castroville for his dedication to growing herbs of extraordinary quality.

Ima Nicefolk was his wife and the mother of his two children. Unlike her husband, she was a jolly soul, always giggling and entertaining the children with funny games and cookies baked with sweet-tasting herbs. A small woman, she fluttered about, like a bird hopping across a lawn.

Then there were Casey and Lacey, who were ten-year-old nonidentical twins, since a boy and a girl cannot be identical. Casey was a blond boy with hair as yellow as marigolds, so his mother told everyone. He had sparkling green eyes that darted all about as if always searching for something. Lacey's hair was golden brown and gleamed like amber under the sun; she had eyes as blue as a robin's eggs.

They all lived in a two-story ranch house under a grove of palm trees without a lawn, since every inch of open ground was devoted to raising prize herbs. The farm was known as Nicefolk Landing because it straddled the Pajaro and Salinas rivers where they ran into the ocean at Monterey Bay. It was a fun place for the children to play—water to swim and row boats in, the rivers filled with fish and turtles and frogs. There was even a nearby railroad track where they could watch the trains roll by and wave to the engineers, who tooted their steam whistles, and to the passengers, who never failed to wave back.

How they longed to board the train and see the country. Neither of the children had been more than twenty miles from the farm. The only times they got away from home were the one- or two-day camping trips they took in the surrounding countryside. There was a great, interesting world out there somewhere, and they wanted someday to see it. If only there was a way.

Casey was not overly fond of school. True, he did well, but he was more interested in exploring and building model airplanes and automobiles, of which he had more than a hundred hanging from the ceiling of his room. He loved all things mechanical and rode around the farm on his little motorized scooter. His teachers often wrote on his report cards, much to the irritation of Mr. Nicefolk, "Casey daydreams and does not apply himself."

Lacey, on the other hand, loved school. She diligently did her homework and excelled in English and mathematics. Outside of school, Lacey created scrumptious recipes with the farm's herbs and designed furniture that Mr. Nicefolk built and sold in town after the herb seeds had been sowed.

When harvesttime came, everybody pitched in to pick the herbs, which was all done by hand without machines. There were no animals on the farm, only a droopy-eyed, long-eared basset hound called Floopy.

After doing his homework, Casey helped his father tend the crops while Lacey helped her mother in the kitchen. Things around the farm seemed normal enough. But lately, there was a strange feeling in the air that seemed to come from the barn.

Barns are fascinating buildings that have their own spirit and soul. This one was built by Grandpa Nicefolk's own hands from stone he had found in the nearby rivers, until the barn was bigger than the house! The sides had arched windows, and the roof had two fanciful cupolas on either end and a weather vane in the shape of an old sailing ship perched on the peak. The interior was huge and open. Beams and braces supported the typical barn roof with a flattened top half and a steep lower half. It was filled with bins where the herbs were stored after they were harvested until the family packed them into sacks for shipping to their buyers.

The scent of the herbs as they dried rose and swirled throughout the barn, mingling to create a hundred different fabulous smells that tickled the noses of all who inhaled the aromas.

People these days avoided the Nicefolk farm as if there was a hex about the place. It was a sense that something was not quite right, like when you get goose bumps on your arms. What almost no one knew, including Mr. and Mrs. Nicefolk, was that the house and field were not hexed. It was the barn that gave off unusual vibrations after a very strange hired hand had left for the harvest season. Those who entered the barn felt their skin tingle. Ever and Ima Nicefolk simply became used to it. Only Casey and Lacey knew the barn's secret.

It all began one year earlier, when a wandering field-worker stopped at the farm. He came down the road between the herb fields, leading a donkey that pulled a small two-wheel wagon whose contents were covered by a red canvas tarpaulin. He came to a halt in the front yard, walked up on the porch and knocked on the door. Floopy came running across the porch, barking in a deep, melodious tone like a foghorn. Suddenly he stopped and walked up to the stranger, sat on his haunches, tilted his head quizzically and stared as a friendly hand stroked him between the ears.

"Most strange," said Mr. Nicefolk, who opened the front door and peered out. "That dog has never taken to a stranger."

"I have a way with animals," said the stranger softly.

"What can I do for you, friend?" asked Mr. Nicefolk.

"I'll help around the farm and work in the field if you can use a good hand."

Mr. Nicefolk shook his head. "Sorry, I can't afford to pay a hired hand. Times are hard, and I have too little acreage to make a profit."

"I won't charge you. I'll work for free except for food and a place to sleep."

Now, Ever Nicefolk was a man who took pride in tending the farm with just his wife and children, but it was an offer he could not refuse, especially since the herbs were due to be harvested in a few days and he needed every cent to feed his family. He was also two months behind on the mortgage on the farm and was afraid the bank might take his hard-worked land away, land that had belonged to his family for four generations.

"Take him on," said Ima Nicefolk, studying the

stranger's body that was as skinny and gaunt as the trunk on a tall palm tree. "He doesn't look like he'll eat much."

An extra pair of hands would be welcome, thought Mr. Nicefolk. A kindly man, he took pity on the stranger, who looked as if he hadn't eaten since last Valentine's Day.

The stranger was unlike any man the twins had ever seen. He was tall, a foot taller than their father, and his rough hands with long, bony fingers hung down nearly to his knees. He was as quick in his movements as Ever Nicefolk was slow. His head turned from side to side, whipping his long gray beard back and forth like a child's swing. But his black eyes stared straight ahead with the intensity of a pair of headlights on a car.

To Lacey and Casey he looked like an understuffed scarecrow.

His appearance wasn't the only thing the Nicefolks found unusual about the curious stranger.

His donkey was as white as one of Mrs. Nicefolk's bedsheets, and the cart the animal was hitched to had been painted a gleaming gold.

When asked his name, the stranger replied, "I'm called Sucoh Sucop."

"That's an odd name," said Ever Nicefolk.

"It's the only one I've got," answered Sucop.

"You can take your meals with me and the family, but you'll have to sleep in the barn. And mind you, don't light any lanterns or candles. I don't want my barn burned down."

Sucop stared at the stone walls and shook his head. "Not much chance of that."

Ever Nicefolk nodded toward the wagon. "I'll give you room and board to bring the herbs to the barn with your wagon and mule."

Sucop smiled and patted the donkey. "Hear that, Mr. Periwinkle? These good folks are going to pay us to bring in their crops from the field."

Mr. Periwinkle lifted his head and brayed.

Then, without another word, Sucop set out for the

barn, followed by Floopy, who had taken an obvious liking to him, and Mr. Periwinkle, who pulled the cart.

Lacey laughed and said, "Didn't any of you recognize his name?"

"It's dumb, that's all I know," said Casey, watching Sucop until he disappeared through the big barn door.

"He's nobody I ever heard of around these parts," Mr. Nicefolk said, shrugging.

"Sucoh Sucop is *hocus pocus* spelled backward," Lacey said triumphantly, having outthought the rest of her family.

Mrs. Nicefolk straightened her apron. "I do declare. No wonder he turned his name around."

Casey was not sure he liked the newcomer. He often thought things out for minutes, sometimes hours and even days, before making up his mind and drawing a logical conclusion. But Casey decided that Mr. Sucop posed no threat and that he would treat him with courtesy. After all, Ever Nicefolk always told his children that courtesy toward others did not cost a nickel.

*Lacey and Casey's eyes were as wide as the dishes
on Mrs. Nicefolk's dinner table.*

2

A Wondrous Thing

For the next two months, Mr. Nicefolk and Sucoh Sucop harvested the herbs and carried them into the barn, then loaded the licorice, spearmint, ginseng and all the other herbs into their special bins until the barn reeked of wonderful smells. Lacey and Casey helped after school, soon becoming friends with Mr. Periwinkle, leading him to the barn with a full load of herbs in the cart and unloading it before bringing him back to the fields for another load. They spent the evening hours after homework listening to wondrous stories by Mr. Sucop, who treated them as if they were his very own children.

The days were warm and comfortable, and the weather cooperated with clear, cloudless skies with no rain, only early morning fog that drifted in during the morning from the ocean. It was the nights that seemed mysterious. After supper, Sucop would go to the barn, where he had wired a small generator to electric lights that shone all night. Soon a mystical glow surrounded the old barn. Neighbors passing on the nearby road often commented about the peculiar phenomenon of light streaming through the barn's windows.

During his spare time when he wasn't laboring in the fields, Sucop disappeared into the barn and didn't come out until dawn. He built an enclosed shop with a large workbench in one corner of the barn. Despite their curiosity, the children were afraid to enter the barn when Sucop was inside. In fact, their father cautioned them to stay away from their field hand to respect his privacy. When they put their ears to the door, which became, oddly, locked except when the herbs were brought in and later packaged, all they could hear were unexplainable tinkling and clinking noises. Then silence, then the tinkling and clinking would resume and go on for an hour at a time before stopping again. They could not begin to guess what their new friend was doing. Even when they were permitted to enter the barn during the workday, they found a big brass padlock on the door of the workshop in the corner with its newly built walls. Whatever was going on inside during the wee hours of the night was most puzzling to the children. They began to suspect that Sucop had a deep, dark secret he did not wish to share with the Nicefolks.

At last, when all the herbs were harvested, packaged and sent to buyers, Sucoh Sucop came to the door one morning and told Mr. Nicefolk that it was time for him to move on.

"Sorry to see you go," said Ever Nicefolk.

"We'll miss you," said Ima Nicefolk.

Lacey and Casey came and stood side by side, petting Mr. Periwinkle for the last time. "Will you come back next harvest season?" asked Casey.

Sucop tugged at his long gray beard and smiled. "I never know where my travels will take me. Mr.

Periwinkle and I simply follow a road until it ends and then take another until that one ends. Should the roads take us in a circle and we arrive back here, we'll be happy to work for you again."

Ever Nicefolk tried to pay Sucop a little money as a bonus, but the man slipped both hands in his pocket, saying, "I can only take what we agreed upon, but thank you kindly." Then he looked down at Lacey and Casey. "Before I leave, there is something I'd like to show you in the barn."

Sucoh Sucop, looking very mysterious, walked into the barn with the children trailing behind him and Floopy loping beside Mr. Periwinkle. Inside, he stopped in front of the locked workshop. Then he dug into his pocket, produced a key and opened the door.

The interior was dark, but he pressed a tiny switch on the wall and the workshop was flooded with a light that shone with all the colors of the rainbow. The workshop was empty of all his para-phernalia—he had loaded all that on his cart. The walls and workbench were clean of tools except a small copper box with two levers protruding from the top. Other than the box, all the children could see was a large, square mat on the floor that shimmered under the mystical light. Sucoh Sucop took a toy out of a pocket on his overalls and placed it on the mat. It was a small hand-carved model of his cart.

"Now watch closely," he said in a measured voice, smiling widely, "and see what you have never seen."

Then he pressed the left lever on the box.

Slowly, very slowly, the little toy cart glimmered and sparkled. Next came a wisp of what looked like purple smoke but was really a heavy mist. The mist swirled and whirled for nearly a minute, then began to scatter in a shower of tiny glittering stars before fading away.

Suddenly, the toy cart seemed to grow and grow until it was as big as Sucop's real cart.

Lacey and Casey's eyes were as wide as the dishes on Mrs. Nicefolk's dinner table. They stood rooted in astonishment before jumping up and down with excitement. Then they began to calm down and wonder if their eyes were playing tricks inside their heads.

Reading their minds, Sucop said, "It's real. Go ahead and touch it."

Lacey was afraid, but Casey, wanting to show his sister that he was brave, approached the cart and cautiously extended his hand until his fingers touched one of the wheels. Quickly he pulled his hand back, then reached out again and ran his hand over the staked sides.

"It *is* real," he gasped. "I can feel it."

Still not fully convinced, Casey abruptly turned and looked toward the barn door. Believing that Sucop had somehow moved his cart into the barn during the mist, he ran outside. There was the cart, still hitched to Mr. Periwinkle, with Floopy sitting next to it, his tongue dangling out one side of his jaw.

Returning as if in a daze, Casey stared at the

second cart, then looked up at Sucop and asked, "How did you do that?"

"Enchantment," Sucop answered easily.

"It must be a magic trick," said Lacey.

Sucop shook his head solemnly. "No trick. I have given you both the secret of enchantment. All you have to do to make a small toy big is set it on the mat and push the left lever of the mystical box. Then you must believe with all your heart that your toy will become as real as life itself."

"What does the right lever do?" Casey wondered, relying on his inquiring mind.

"That one makes the object tiny again. Just watch." He touched the lever, and in a puff of purple haze, the cart became little again.

Lacey threw her arms around Sucop—actually her arms couldn't quite reach around his waist—and hugged him. "Thank you, thank you for such a wonderful gift."

Casey, trying to act grown up, shook Sucop's hand. "How can we ever thank you?"

Sucop smiled. "Use the gift only for good and it will last you a lifetime. But if you use it for bad, it will vanish in a puff of red smoke."

"No, no," the children cried in unison. "We will never use it for wicked things."

"And remember, when you are finished with whatever toy you alter, you can make it small again."

"And if we don't, will it last forever and ever?" asked Lacey.

"Then it will remain real," Sucop assured her. "And one other thing. This is our secret. No one else must ever learn the magic."

"Not even our mother and father?"

Sucop ran his hand through her golden hair. "Not even your mother and father, or the spell will disappear, never to return. Love and cherish the secret and it will last until you're both grown up."

"Not after?" asked Casey.

Sucop slowly shook his head. "Then your dreams will take new directions, and the secret will fade in your mind and heart."

With that, he spun on his heels and walked from the barn. He never turned and looked back as he and Mr. Periwinkle set off down the road.

Lacey and Casey watched with tears of sadness in their eyes until their friend passed through the fields and became lost to their sight.

Finally, Lacey turned to Casey. "What should we do now?" she asked, wiping away her tears.

Casey thought a moment, then his eyes brightened and a wide grin spread across his face. "Let's see if we can make the magic work. I have an idea. You wait here."

Casey ran off to the house. A few minutes later, he returned. In one hand he held a small red toy tractor that he had played with in a sandbox behind the back porch. "We'll make a real tractor for Father and tell him it came from Mr. Sucop."

Lacey clapped her hands. "How wonderful. Father will be so pleased, and he'll have something to remember Mr. Sucop by."

"It's the least we can do," said Casey.

Quickly, they placed the little tractor, with its little yellow wheels on the front and big wheels on the back, on the magical mat. There was a tiny steering wheel and a little seat for the driver. The engine that could be seen under the open hood was painted silver.

Casey took the copper box and stared at Lacey. "You ready?"

"Yes, yes. Are you sure you know which lever to push?"

"He said the left one."

Nervous and gripped by suspense, Casey pushed the lever and held his breath. As with the cart, the tiny tractor glimmered and sparkled, followed by the thick, swirling, whirling purple mist.

But nothing happened. The toy tractor was still a toy tractor.

"You must have pushed the wrong lever," said Lacey.

Casey shook his head. "No, something doesn't work. Maybe it *was* a trick."

"Mr. Sucop said we must believe with all our hearts. That has to be it. We didn't believe. Let's try again, but this time we must have faith that the tractor will grow into a real one."

They closed their eyes and wished and wished and wished with all their hearts that the little tractor would grow into a big one. They did not see the mist or the miniature burst of stars or hear anything but a cooing dove nesting in the rafters far above them. After a full minute, they slowly opened their eyes.

There in the middle of the barn on the magical mat sat a life-size red tractor with yellow wheels.

Lacey and Casey gazed with joy and rapture at the vehicle. As if in a trance, they walked around it, studying every bolt, every nut and screw, feeling the brown leather on the seat and the gleaming radiator cap with its round thermometer behind a small glass viewing window.

"We did it!" Lacey exclaimed. "The magical box works just as Mr. Sucop said it would."

Casey climbed onto the tractor and settled in the brown leather seat and gripped the big steering wheel. "I wonder if it really runs."

"Do you know how to start it?"

Casey nodded as if the question irritated him. "Of course. It's simple. You turn on the ignition switch, pull out the choke and press the starter button." He did all three and the starter motor whirred as it turned over the big four-cylinder engine. And then there came a roar up the vertical exhaust pipe through the muffler, and the engine began to thump on all four cylinders. A funny little hinged cap that kept water out when it rained flipped up and down on top of the exhaust pipe.

Casey acted as if this was an everyday routine and beamed like a lighthouse. "Come along, Lacey, and we'll drive it up to the house so Mother and Father can see it."

"Not me. Are you sure you can drive this thing?" she asked skeptically. "Your feet barely touch the pedals."

"I told you, it's simple. I only have to shift it into gear and let out the clutch." Saying that, Casey could barely push in the clutch with his toe. Next, he pressed his other foot down on the gas pedal. Having forgotten to straighten the steering wheel, he watched in horror as the tractor leaped forward and crashed through the barn door.

Now really worried, Lacey ran through the hole in the barn door after the tractor as it lurched toward the house. Frantically, Casey pushed the gear level into neutral and pushed the brake with all his might. The tractor came to a stop not five feet from the front porch steps. Ima Nicefolk was in the middle of fixing dinner, and Ever Nicefolk was washing his face and hands after planting herbs all morning. They heard the noise from the crash and came running out on the porch just in time to see Casey climb down off the tractor, his face etched in fright. Dumbfounded, the Nicefolks could not comprehend where the tractor had come from. It was as if it had appeared out of nowhere.

Mr. Nicefolk asked, "Where did that come from?"

And Mrs. Nicefolk asked, "Who does it belong to?"

Casey said, "It is a gift from Mr. Sucop."

And Lacey said, "Isn't it beautiful? It's ours now."

Mr. Nicefolk shook his head in wonderment. "Mr. Sucop gave this to us? I can't believe it. He had no money to buy such a fancy machine. He must have stolen it."

"Oh no," the twins shouted as one. "He didn't steal it. We know."

"He made it from parts of other tractors," Casey said, pleased that he didn't lie.

"Are you children certain of this?" asked Mr. Nicefolk.

"Oh yes," they chimed together. "He worked on it at night in the shop he built in the barn."

Ever Nicefolk shrugged and turned to his wife. "Well, then, I guess we have to thank Mr. Sucop for working all those hours at night to make a new tractor we can use in the fields from now on."

The Nicefolks loved their tractor. Mr. Nicefolk drove it up and down the road and to town to show it off to his friends and neighbors. Neither he nor Mrs. Nicefolk ever noticed that Casey never played with his little tractor in the sandbox again. Nor did they notice that it was gone.

*Casey took hold of one of the long paddlelike
propeller blades and pulled it around.*

3

The Magical *Vin Fiz*

Lacey and Casey did not use the magical box to make any toys grow big during the next two months. They were afraid to overdo the enchantment and decided to save it for only those times when it might be needed.

The spring harvest had come and gone. Summer had arrived, and school was out. During the warm, sunny days, they played in the fields, swam in the rivers and floated on air mattresses their father had bought them from a sporting goods store in town. They also fished and were often successful in catching catfish that they brought home for dinner.

One early morning, before the rooster crowed and while the eastern sky was just beginning to brighten, Casey crept into Lacey's room and woke her up.

"What is it?" she asked sleepily. "What are you doing up so early?"

"Get up and get dressed," he whispered. "I've got something I want to show you."

"What about Mother and Father?"

"I don't want them to know."

Not understanding and her mind fogged from sleep, Lacey dressed and followed her brother quietly down the stairs to the living room, out the door to the porch and across the yard to the barn. Their father had repaired the door that Casey had crashed the tractor through, and it looked as good as new. Floopy trailed behind, yawning from being awakened so early.

The red tractor with the yellow wheels sat in one corner of the barn, all clean and shiny. Mr. Nicefolk always wiped the dust off after he drove it and kept it as neat as the inside of Mrs. Nicefolk's oven.

"Now, what is so secret you have to drag me down here in the wee hours of the morning?" demanded Lacey.

Without answering, Casey stepped over to the workbench built by Sucoh Sucop, where an unseen object was sitting under a cloth. He lifted off the cloth and held up the object.

"What is it?" asked Lacey.

"A model of a Wright brothers airplane," he replied. "I built it myself."

She moved closer and studied the little model as Casey held it in the air. In her mind, it was funny looking. It didn't look anything like the airplanes that flew over the house. It had the appearance of an old antique that could never get off the ground. She stared at the two wings and the quaint engine. Two narrow chains ran in pulleys from the engine that turned the propellers. The wings and control surfaces were painted a bright yellow with green letters. It rolled on two sets of two wheels attached to skilike runners that stuck out in front of the airplane.

"What does the lettering say?" she asked.

"Its name."

"And what do you call it?"

Casey looked proudly at his work. "I named it *Vin Fiz* after my favorite grape soda pop."

"What a goofy name," said Lacey. "What are you going to do with it?"

"Make a big one, of course."

"But why?"

Casey looked at his sister as if his mind was made up. "So we can fly it across the country and see all the sights we've only dreamed about."

Before Lacey could protest or complain, he put the little model on the magical pad. She stopped him just as he was about to press the lever.

"Wait!" she said loudly.

"What's wrong?" Casey asked, surprised.

"The wings," she answered. "If you make it full size, we'll never get it through the door out of the barn."

Casey looked at his sister with deep respect. "You're right," he admitted.

He took the little model and the mystic pad outside and laid them on the grass. Then he pressed the left lever and wished with all his might. Now the twins believed in the magic of the box with all their hearts.

After the expected display of mist and lights, a life-size Wright brothers airplane in all its glory materialized (which means it became a reality). It glowed in the dawn sun.

Lacey stood in amazement. "Surely, you don't expect to fly that thing."

"I most certainly do," answered Casey. "I even built a seat for you and a box where we can carry Floopy."

"When did you learn to fly?" she asked sarcastically.

"I looked at the pictures in a manual published by the Wright brothers that tells all about how to fly their airplane. Besides, I feel most certain that an enchanted airplane will almost fly herself. Now help me push her onto the road."

"Her?"

"Sure, airplanes and boats are always called *she* and *her*. Why not *he* and *him* I'll never know."

As big and bulky as *Vin Fiz* seemed, she was light and rolled quite smoothly on her four wheels and skids. The wings easily passed between the palm trees lining the road. It was almost as if the magical box had known what size the plane should be. As they pushed, Floopy walked around and sniffed at the engine with its smell of oil and gasoline. Lacey could not be sure, but she thought that Floopy seemed to look forward to the flight.

The sun was just poking above the herb fields like a big orange ball when Casey suddenly thought of something. "I almost forgot. I'll be right back." He hurried to the house, quietly ran up the stairs to his bedroom and took five dollars he had saved from a piggy bank he kept in his closet. Next he rushed into the kitchen, opened the refrigerator door and removed a bottle. When he returned, he held it up and showed the purple soda inside. "A Vin Fiz for *Vin Fiz*," he said proudly, tying the bottle to one of the wing struts. "Now, everybody in," he ordered as he lifted Floopy onto a pillow inside the dog's carrying box.

"I'm not sure I want to do this," Lacey said hesitantly. She stared uneasily at the thin wooden struts and thin fabric on the wings and control surfaces. "She seems too flimsy to fly."

"Don't be a scaredy-cat." Casey laughed. "She's perfectly safe. You'll see."

"How do we start her?"

"I'll spin one of the propellers to get the cylinders firing. You work the throttle that feeds gas to the engine."

Against her better judgment, Lacey sat in one seat and found the throttle. Next she turned the little lever that turned the ignition switch to ON. "Ready when you are," she announced, still fearful of flying in such an odd machine.

Casey took hold of one of the long paddlelike propeller blades and pulled it around. There was a brief sputter and then nothing. He pulled it around again and again. Nothing. Finally, he yanked it with all his strength and the engine popped once, twice, three times and began to fire on all four cylinders.

Pleased that everything was working as he hoped, Casey ran around the plane and jumped into the pilot's seat. He gave Lacey a leather helmet with goggles for herself and one for Floopy. Next, he pulled his helmet down over his head and adjusted the goggles over his eyes. "Fasten your seat belt and see that Floopy is secure in his box," he told her.

The engine rattled and clanked at first before it warmed up. Then it smoothed out and the exhaust sounded like *poppity-pop-pop.* The plane had no brakes, so Casey simply moved the throttle and the plane began to roll down the road. Surprisingly, Ever and Ima Nicefolk slept through the loud noise out in the yard. Ima always kept the bedroom windows closed because she did not like the damp air blowing in from the nearby ocean.

Very slowly at first, the Wright *Flyer,* as it was originally called, crept forward. Soon *Vin Fiz* picked up speed and moved faster and faster. Casey gripped the controls, two vertical levers that rose up on both sides of his seat. The wind began whistling through the struts and spars and wires as the airplane sped over the bumpy dirt road. Then Casey pulled back on the control levers and *Vin Fiz* leaped into the air, leaving a great cloud of dust behind her.

The buildings and automobiles looked so small, they seemed like little toys that she could pluck from the streets.

4

The Long Journey Begins

Higher and higher *Vin Fiz* soared, until the herb fields fell away like a green blanket pulled over the end of a bed. Casey and Lacey leaped from a two-dimensional world on the ground into a third dimension of sky and space. Now they could travel up or down in any direction they desired. Lacey's heart beat so quickly that she thought it would burst through her chest as Casey flew over the little hamlet of Castroville. The buildings and automobiles looked so small, they seemed like little toys that she could pluck from the streets. The buildings and houses looked tiny too. For the first time she could see the rooftops. To the people on the ground who stared up when they heard the sound of the engine's exhaust, the Wright *Flyer* appeared as a yellow bird against a brilliant blue sky, highlighted by a vibrant golden sun.

At first the airplane dipped and swung from side to side until Casey became more familiar with the controls. Soon he had her leveled off and smoothly sailing through the air as if he'd been flying for years. He circled over Castroville and then headed west toward the Pacific Ocean only a mile away. They flew over a wide, white sandy beach, lapped by green waves rolling in from the sea. The water and sky blended into vibrant blue as radiant as a vast sapphire. A flock of seagulls appeared and flew alongside *Vin Fiz*, staring curiously through beady eyes at the strange man-made machine that flew in their sky. Floopy barked at them, but they could hardly hear him over the noise of the engine and thump of the propellers. Unable to identify the odd bird in their midst, they winged away and dove toward the water in search of a meal.

Lacey's heartbeat became normal again as her fear ebbed, and she began to enjoy the ride. "Where are we going?" she shouted over the rattle of the exhaust.

"We're going to fly cross-country to New York," Casey yelled back.

"Isn't that an awfully long way?"

"Yes, but we should always look over the next horizon to see what's beyond."

"How do we know how to get there?" she inquired in growing disbelief.

Casey took a folded piece of paper from his pocket and handed it to her. "Here's a map. While I fly, you navigate."

"What will Mother and Father say when we don't show up for breakfast?"

Casey smiled. "I left a note on my pillow telling them we would be gone for a while on a little camping trip. They won't mind. We've done it enough times."

"But we never went farther than a mile," Lacey protested. "I don't think of going to New York as *a little camping trip.*"

"*Vin Fiz* is fast," he replied. "We'll be home before you know it."

She reached into her pocket and pulled out a small red leather book with a pencil. "Lucky I brought my diary so I can record events," she said, getting in the mood of the adventure.

Casey banked the airplane and set a course toward the northeast. The fields of artichokes spread out below them like a vast carpet. Then came the farms of the San Joaquin Valley, and before they knew it, they were flying over the Sierra Nevada Mountains into Yosemite National Park. Lacey and Casey stared in awe at the spectacular scenery, the high, sheer rock cliffs of Half Dome and El Capitan that rose above a flat valley filled with colorful wildflowers, all in vivid bloom. They flew past Yosemite and Bridalveil falls, whose streams of water fell hundreds of feet to the valley floor in a white spray accompanied by colorful rainbows.

Floopy barked at a bear that looked up at them and a herd of mule deer that ran, frightened by the strange bird with its loud engine exhaust that echoed back and forth across the valley between the rock walls. A golden eagle flew alongside them for a few miles, gracefully gliding above *Vin Fiz* before diving down into the valley.

Then they were over the giant sequoia trees that towered three hundred feet from the ground. The largest of all living things, they had endured for thousands of years.

After leaving the mountains, Casey swooped down into the Mojave Desert and on into Nevada. The flowering shrubs, oak woodlands, pine and cedar trees were left behind as the land turned brown and green plants faded away. All they could see were miles and miles of vast dry flatlands, broken only by occasional rocky hills that rose above a few clumps of sagebrush. There was little between them and the horizon but a barren wilderness.

"I'm hungry," cried Lacey.

"Already? It's not even noon yet."

"We didn't have any breakfast."

"Look for a nearby town on your map so we can land and find us a place to eat."

She unfolded the map and found a little town that sat alone in the middle of the desert. "Turn to the right. There is a town very close."

Casey pointed ahead. "I see it—there, at the foot of that big hill."

While he tenderly jockeyed with the control levers, *Vin Fiz* acted as if she had a mind of her own and began gliding gradually downward onto the main street of the town. It was little more than a wide dirt road; there was no pavement to be seen. The wheels touched gently onto the ground. The airplane rolled less than fifty feet down the middle of the street before stopping in front of a big two-story wooden building with an overhead sign that read GOLD CITY HOTEL. As they lifted their goggles and gazed around the town, they found it very strange that no one appeared to gawk at the sight of an airplane sitting on the main street. There was an unexplainable silence about the place. Even Floopy seemed subdued and did not bark.

"Where are all the people?" wondered Lacey.

"It looks deserted," said Casey.

"I find it awfully spooky."

"I know," said Casey, acting suddenly enlightened. "We must have landed smack-dab in the middle of an old ghost town."

And yet it did not look like an old, dilapidated or run-down ghost town. The boardwalks in front of the buildings were clean, and there was no litter in the street. True, the schoolhouse and the church looked badly in need of repair, as did the city hall and town jail, but the houses appeared neat and freshly painted.

Lacey unclasped her seat belt, jumped from the airplane and walked over to a window of a merchandise store and peered in. "The shelves and counters are stocked with goods," she reported. Then she cautiously stepped to the front door and took one step, no more, inside. New kitchen utensils were displayed, all clean and shiny. Clothes hung on racks, and cans of grocery items were stacked neatly on the shelves. She saw no sign of the dust or cobwebs that one might think would be found in an abandoned ghost town.

It was all very eerie.

Casey pointed to a sign advertising a café next to the hotel. "Maybe we can find something to eat over there."

"If not, the store looks like it has canned food," she said.

Floopy was not behaving like he was happy and about to be fed. He sniffed the air with his enormous nose and raised his huge floppy ears to listen. He did not act like a cheery dog. He definitely sensed something that mere humans could not. He sensed trouble.

Becoming a bit braver, Lacey and Casey entered the café and looked around. The chairs were all neatly parked under the tables. Silverware was laid out next to dishes on blue tablecloths, just like on their dining table at home. The napkin holders and salt and pepper shakers were all in order, as if expecting diners to arrive at any minute. Timidly, they sat down at a table and picked up menus.

"I'd love to eat a hamburger," said Casey.

Lacey began to read her menu. "I'm so hungry, I could eat everything in the kitchen."

At the mention of the word *kitchen,* they turned and stared at the swinging doors that led into the kitchen from the dining room. Kitchens always had swinging doors so the waiters and waitresses could walk in and out carrying dishes without reaching for a door handle.

"Hello!" Casey called out. "Anyone out there?"

No answer came.

Warily, they rose from the table, walked over and peeked under the swinging doors. The cooking area of the café was deserted. A big black iron stove stood cold and empty of pots and pans. The metal counters were clean and bright. The sinks were empty of dirty dishes, and the trays of knives, forks and spoons looked freshly washed.

"Where did everyone go?" Lacey asked as if lost in a dream.

"As soon as we make ourselves some lunch," Casey said, opening a walk-in icebox, "we're going to find out."

Lacey fixed her brother with a questioning gaze. "Do you mind if I ask how we're going to pay?"

He reached into his pants pocket and held up five folded one-dollar bills. "I borrowed from my piggy bank for just such an emergency."

Finding what they wanted in the big icebox and a pantry, they made cheese and ham sandwiches with mayonnaise, mustard, lettuce and tomato. For drinks they found a small pitcher filled with milk. Since they were half starved, it all tasted good, so good that they had to use their utmost self-control to keep from making more sandwiches.

But Casey looked at the menu and declared, "We have eaten up a dollar's worth of ham and cheese sandwiches with two glasses of milk. We can't take more without paying more."

"That's all right," said Lacey. "I'm full anyway."

They left the dollar on the table under the saltshaker and walked back out onto the wooden sidewalk. Then they looked up and down the street as fear and shock mushroomed inside them.

The middle of the street was as empty as a bedroom without a bed, as empty as a tool shed without tools, even emptier than a mountain stream without water.

Vin Fiz was gone. She had disappeared, vanished and evaporated as though she had never existed.

Suddenly, three very tall men,
at least they looked very tall to a pair of ten-year-olds,
came near and glared down at the children.

5

The Bad Guys

"She's not here!" Lacey cried. "Someone has taken *Vin Fiz!*"

Floopy frantically ran around the spot where he'd last seen the airplane and raised his nose toward the sky. Then he began to circle, using his big, black nose like the needle pointing on a compass. Catching the scent, he gave off a howl and began running down the street toward the big hill beyond the town. Both Lacey and Casey gave chase.

Though not nearly as fast as a greyhound or even a dachshund, who could run rings around a basset hound, Floopy's short, stubby legs could carry him miles and miles without tiring. He soon left Lacey and Casey far behind.

"Oh no," cried Lacey, "we've lost Floopy."

"We'll catch him," Casey said confidently. "Look down. All we have to do is follow the tracks."

Staring down onto the dirt road, Lacey could see Floopy's paw prints over the wheel ruts of *Vin Fiz*. Casey pointed to hoof marks also pressed into the soft dirt. "Whoever stole our airplane towed it away with a horse."

They ran, following the trail until the tracks disappeared when the dirt road turned into a rock road that seemed to travel in all directions. "Oh no," Lacey cried again, searching in vain for a sign of the trail. "Now we'll never find Floopy or *Vin Fiz*."

"Don't worry, Sis. Look closer."

Lacey knelt down and studied the rock. There, before her eyes, as plain as the tips of her fingers, was a trail of black oil drops that traveled on toward the big hill outside of town. She looked up and laughed. "*Vin Fiz* is leaving a trail so we can find her."

"I told you she was enchanted," Casey said, puffing out his chest with an "I told you so" expression on his face. "And when we find her, we'll find Floopy. Come on, let's hurry."

The twins raced across the flat sea of rocks, following the trail of oil. As they got closer to the big hill, they came onto railroad tracks. These were not your ordinary wide railroad tracks with long ties and thick steel rails. This track was just a little over a foot wide from rail to rail.

"What sort of train runs on these narrow rails?" questioned Casey.

"Remember the train we rode on in the park when Father took us to the Castroville carnival last summer?" Lacey asked. "It had small rails too. They called it a narrow gauge."

They followed the track until it came to a huge pile of rock that fell off down the hill. Two rusty iron cars in the shape of large buckets stood on the rails that ended at the top of the rock pile. The bucket cars were attached together by what Casey recognized as couplings and were filled with rocks.

"They're ore carts," said Lacey.

"How do you know?"

"I saw them in a picture book on gold mining. They're used to haul ore dug from mines."

Then Casey's eyes followed the twin rails into the hillside and he saw it. No more than a hundred feet away and no less than ninety feet away was the entrance to a cave whose mouth yawned menacingly.

"The oil trail leads into that cave," he declared in a hushed voice.

Slowly, holding hands, they walked until they had entered the cave. It widened into a cavern as big as their barn back home.

Joyously, the children clapped their hands and shouted with glee. "*Vin Fiz*! There's *Vin Fiz*!"

And so she was.

The yellow airplane with the green lettering sat in the center of the cave, as good as the day she had materialized, which, of course, was that same day.

But something was wrong. Lacey immediately realized what it was.

"Floopy isn't here," she moaned. "I don't see him anywhere."

Casey nodded toward an opening in one wall, where the narrow-gauge railroad entered. "He must have run in there."

They approached what they recognized as the entrance to a mine shaft. Suddenly, three very tall men, at least they looked very tall to a pair of ten-year-olds, came near and glared down at the children. The one who stood in front of the other two was dressed like an old Western gunslinger, with his Colt revolver hung in a holster on his belt. A black hat covered an oily mange of hair and a huge walrus mustache spread across his upper lip. He wore a black shirt tucked into black pants tucked into black boots. His henchmen—they had to be his henchmen since he acted like a boss—were also dressed in black Western clothes. The twins were both relieved and fearful to see one of the men holding Floopy, who was whining with a muzzle around his nose and jaws.

The one clutching Floopy under one arm hissed at the man in front of him, "I told you they'd show up, Boss, after we stole their airplane."

"Yeah," said the other henchman, grinning. "It was my idea."

"No it wasn't. It was mine."

"Was not."

"Was too."

"Not."

"Too."

"You're both wrong," snapped the Boss. "I thought of it. Now be quiet."

The two henchmen hunched their shoulders and cowered at the Boss's cold voice.

The Boss glared down at the children and growled, "And where did you two little scamps pop up from? And who sent you?"

"Nobody sent us." Casey stepped in front of his sister since she was trembling so much, she could hardly stand. "We flew here"—he paused and pointed toward *Vin Fiz*—"in our airplane, from Castroville."

"Castroville," snorted the Boss. "Never heard of it."

"It happens to be in California," Lacey said indignantly, feeling a little braver.

Then he stared at *Vin Fiz*. "You flew here in that old pile of junk?"

"It's not a pile of junk," Lacey said angrily. "It's an enchanted airplane."

It was obvious the Boss saw nothing enchanted about the plane. "Does anyone know you're here?"

Casey shook his head. "We didn't tell anybody where we were going."

"And just where were you going?"

"New York," answered Lacey.

The Boss looked at them like they had just arrived from the moon. Then an evil grin spread across his face. "You won't be going to New York anytime soon." He turned to his henchmen. "Let's show them their new home."

The Boss and his henchmen began laughing like hyenas as the Boss led the way into the mine shaft. As soon as they were inside, their laughter echoed off the rock walls and rolled deep down the tunnel into the hill. The twins had to be careful not to trip over the wooden railroad ties holding the narrow-gauge iron tracks together. The henchman carrying Floopy dropped him roughly to the ground and began dragging him with a leash. Floopy gamely dug his paws into the rocky tunnel floor but was dragged along despite his struggles.

"Don't give me a hard time," barked the henchman.

Soon they came to a massive iron gate that blocked further entry into the tunnel. The Boss produced a key and unlatched a bronze lock. Then he swung the gate open just as an ore cart appeared from the other side pushed by two young girls not much older than Casey and Lacey. The girls were dressed in ragged and dirty dresses. They looked very tired from pushing the heavy cart, which was piled high with rock ore. One of the Boss's henchmen was in back, prodding them on with a long stick.

"Move it, girlie girls, we've got six more loads to dump before you can have your beans and water."

Floopy tried to bark through his muzzle. The Boss twisted one of the dog's long ears and sneered. "Save your strength, you stupid mutt. You'll be hitched to one of those ore carts before you know it."

Lacey slapped the Boss's hand away from Floopy's ear. "You leave my dog alone," she said stoutly.

The Boss's eyes glinted like the devil for a moment before he saw the humor in the brave girl's actions. "You're going to work for me, little girlie. I can use someone with your grit."

The twins did not like what was happening to them, did not like it at all. Their tummies were flip-flopping with dread of what might happen to them at the hands of the Boss. There was little they could do, only wait and see what would happen next.

What happened was that they walked into another huge cavern with a high rock dome. Over a hundred people were laboring with picks and shovels, loading rock into the ore carts. Men and boys wielded the picks and filled the little rusty carts while the women and girls pushed them through the tunnel to the dump outside. Some dragged a big wheel-like stone that crushed the ore before it was panned with water for gold.

In as grown-up a voice as he could rally, Casey demanded, "Why were we brought here, and who are all these people?"

"Ho, ho, snoopy, are we?" The Boss leaned down

and leered nastily. "You were brought here because we couldn't let you go and tell the world that my men and I have rounded up all the townspeople and are forcing them to work as slaves mining gold so my comrades and I can all become as rich as kings."

"But there are more of them than you," said Lacey. "Why don't they band together and overpower you and your goons?"

The Boss did not like the word *goons,* so he stepped on Lacey's foot as he answered and made her wince. "Because we kidnapped all their children and are keeping them prisoner in another area of the mine. If they do not work, then . . ." The Boss shrugged, and the message became clear to the twins.

"You wouldn't dare hurt children," said Casey firmly.

"Only cowards would harm little children," chimed in Lacey.

"If threats make these fools mine for gold, so be it."

"The police will catch you," Lacey said angrily.

The Boss laughed from deep inside his belly. "Hardy, har, har. The police, you say. For your information, there isn't a cop within five days' ride from here. A troop of U.S. Cavalry is stationed at Fort Blodgett a good twenty miles away, but they have no idea what is going on. Old Colonel Rumby, the commandeer, rides into town only once every two months." He paused and counted on his fingers. "He's not due for another five weeks. By then, we'll be long gone, with all the gold we can carry. Enough to keep us in a rich man's lifestyle for the rest of our lives."

Casey said curtly, "Thieves never live well."

The Boss turned to his henchmen. "Only smart thieves like us. Right, boys?"

Cruel men, all the henchmen within hearing cheered and laughed and clapped their hands, envisioning their newfound and stolen wealth.

"Now it's time for you two to earn your keep," said the Boss. He nodded to a henchman with fat lips and an ugly flat nose the size of a teacup. "Put 'em to work loading the ore carts. And don't feed them until they load ten."

Casey opened his mouth to protest, but the Boss made a movement of drawing his finger across his throat. The signal sent a shiver through Casey, and he remained silent.

"Not a word out of you," snapped the Boss. "Now off to work."

Casey ignored him. "What about our dog? Leave him with us."

The Boss's lip curled. "Not a chance. I'll keep him tied to my bunk. If you don't work hard, I'll have my boys cook and eat him."

The Boss laughed a rotten laugh when he saw the twins' horrified looks. He turned his back and walked away as one of his henchmen, a man with a scar across his cheek and yellow teeth from never having brushed them, hustled the children off to a narrow-gauge track. There five ore carts sat next to a large pile of crushed ore. "Start filling these up if you young 'uns know what's good for ya."

So Lacey and Casey began shoveling the crushed rock ore that had been washed free of all traces of gold. As they shoveled, they could see two of the Boss's henchmen carefully scooping up the gold dust and pouring it into leather sacks that were then laid end to end along one corner of the mine. Casey counted at least thirty sacks.

"There must be a fortune in gold in those sacks," he said, marveling at such riches.

"It doesn't belong to the Boss," Lacey said indignantly. "It belongs to all the townspeople."

A man and a woman approached. Both were dirty with torn and ragged clothes. He had been lifting heavy rock onto the crusher, and she had been pushing an ore cart. They looked warily at the henchmen to make sure they were not observed as they passed by the twins. They stopped and made as if they were working and spoke softly.

"How did you come to be captured by the Boss?" the man asked. He was tall and lanky with kindly blue eyes.

"We flew into town from Castroville and stopped for something to eat," Lacey answered.

"What are your names?"

Casey answered, "I'm Casey Nicefolk, and this is my twin sister, Lacey."

"It's not right for children so young to be loading ore carts," spoke the nice lady, who was not much taller than the twins. She had long red hair that hung down to her waist, and her eyes gleamed dark green.

"Are you from the town?" asked Lacey.

"I am Stoke Firepit, and this is my wife, Blaze. I'm the mayor of Gold City, or least I was until the Boss and his henchmen came to town and rounded up all the citizens. They brought us here and put everyone to work making them rich."

"He said you didn't fight because he took your children."

The mayor nodded. "Before we knew and could resist, they had captured all the children along with their teacher at the schoolhouse and imprisoned them deep in the mine. We had no choice but to do as they ordered. They threatened to harm the boys and girls."

"Has anyone tried to escape and go to Fort Blodgett for help?" asked Casey.

The mayor shook his head. "We'd be on foot and they have horses. We wouldn't get very far before they ran us down."

Lacey and Casey looked at each other and smiled knowingly. "We could get to the fort without being caught," Casey informed the mayor and his tiny wife.

"Not possible for you youngsters to outrun horses," the mayor whispered as a henchman walked past, prodding a pair of young ladies to push a loaded ore cart. While they walked by, Blaze Firepit made a show of shoveling ore while her husband lifted a rock and heaved it toward the crusher. Intrigued, he asked, "What have you got in mind?"

"We have an airplane," Casey informed them. "Lacey and I could fly to the fort."

"Airplane?" questioned the mayor skeptically.

"Didn't you hear them, dear? They said they flew in from Castroville."

"I've never heard of Castroville."

"It's in California," Lacey informed him. "It's where they grow artichokes."

The mayor was not an optimistic man by nature. He always looked on the downside and rarely looked up. But he was also a logical man, who liked to consider every possibility. "Where is this airplane of yours?"

"In the main cavern before you enter the mine shaft. The Boss had it towed from town after we landed."

The mayor went into deep thought, as he did before he made any decision. Then he shrugged.

"No, no, no. There is no way to escape from the mine. You'd be caught long before you reached your airplane."

"If you don't try," Lacey said sensibly, "you don't do. If you don't do, you don't achieve. And if you don't achieve, you don't succeed. That's what my father always says. So we must find a way."

Mrs. Firepit was not as logical as her husband, but she was more creative. "Why not hide them in an ore cart?" she suggested grandly.

"Yes, yes," Lacey said excitedly. "You could cover us with the ore. Then after we're pushed out of the mine shaft, the ladies who are pushing the cart can dump us onto the ore pile. The henchmen guarding the cart probably won't be watching very closely something they've seen many times."

"They have a point," said Blaze Firepit.

"Could be," mused her husband. "The children are small enough to lie on the bottom of the cart." He interrupted himself and looked to see if any hench-men might be watching or listening. But none paid

68

them any attention. Without any further gloomy thoughts involving logic, he said, "If the Boss and his men catch you, they will be very mad."

"Once we're in *Vin Fiz,* they'll never catch us," said Casey firmly.

"When I give the word, jump into the cart. All set?"

Lacey and Casey each moved around and crouched behind an ore cart. After a minute that seemed an eternity, Mayor Firepit hissed loudly, "Now!"

Then came a clanking sound as the ore cart buckets were
turned on their sides and the load of finely crushed ore,
along with Lacey and Casey, spilled out down the dump pile.

6

Escape to Fort Blodgett

Lacey and Casey did not shilly-shally. They both leaped into an ore cart as quick as you could say "jump in the ore cart."

The Firepits wasted no time in shoveling the ore from the crushing machine that had been cleaned of all gold. It was as fine as plain dirt. Most all boys enjoy playing in the dirt. Casey thought it fun as it was thrown on top of him, until he was covered completely with only his nose sticking up. Not so Lacey. She saw nothing fun about getting all dirty. She felt plain awful about being buried in the damp earth.

After the last shovelful, Mayor Firepit leaned into the cars and said softly, "Try not to move or make a sound until you are emptied on the dirt heap outside. Fly due east until you see the fort. Good luck to you, children."

"Our prayers go with you," murmured Mrs. Firepit.

One of the Boss's henchmen, seeing the ore carts were full, rudely shoved a pair of young girls onto the narrow-gauge track. "Start pushing if you want to get fed," he snarled.

The girls, not knowing Lacey and Casey were hidden under the crushed ore, leaned against the carts and began shoving them up the track. Lacey and Casey could not see because their eyes were closed under the dirt. They could hear the poor girls panting and groaning as they manhandled the heavy carts along the track. A short time later they felt the carts stop. Then came a clanking sound as the ore cart buckets were turned on their sides and the load of finely crushed ore, along with Lacey and Casey, spilled out down the dump pile.

The girls saw the children tumble down the slope and were surprised. But they quickly realized an escape attempt was in the making, whispered "good luck" and began pushing the carts back into the mine. Lacey had been right. The henchman stood back in utter boredom and did not bother to glance down at Lacey and Casey, who were now sitting up, brushing the dirt from their eyes and mouths. Instead he simply yawned and commanded the young ladies to hurry up and haul out another load of dirt.

As soon as they were alone, the twins scrambled up the dump pile and ran to *Vin Fiz,* still sitting undisturbed in the center of the cavern. "The bad men can't help but hear the engine when we start it," said Casey. "They'll come running."

But his fear soon faded because the airplane started its engine all by itself in almost complete silence before they even reached her. Flames came from the exhaust pipes, but miraculously, there was no sound. They leaped into their seats, threw on their helmets and goggles and tightened their belts.

"*Vin Fiz* truly is enchanted," cried Lacey joyously.

Casey did not have to put his hands on the control levers or touch the throttle. *Vin Fiz* simply rolled forward out of the cavern, turned her wheels onto the road and raced ahead, lifting into the air as lightly as a butterfly.

For the first time Casey discovered that he no longer had to fly the plane. She flew herself. All he had to do was give her voice commands. "Turn due east," he said, and *Vin Fiz* gently banked in that direction. "And go fast." She responded with a surge from her engine that turned the big propellers like whirlwinds, sending the airplane soaring through the sky at over fifty miles an hour. They flew less than a hundred feet above the sandy desert, sailing over thousands of sagebrush with silver stems and yellow flowers, yuccas with their bundles of purplish-white bell-shaped blossoms and groves of Joshua trees, some standing as tall as forty feet with spiked leaves and creamy-green flowers.

"The desert is so beautiful," Lacey said in a normal voice because *Vin Fiz* was flying so quietly, the only sounds came from the wind humming past the wing struts. She had always thought of the desert as dry and barren, but now she marveled at the vast fields of wildflowers.

"Do you see Fort Blodgett yet?" Casey asked as he kept a wary eye to their rear for any signs of pursuit from the Boss and his henchmen.

She raised her goggles and shielded her eyes from the sun. "I see it, I see it," she cried with excitement. "I can make out the walls and guard towers on the corners."

It wasn't long before *Vin Fiz* was circling the stars-and-stripes flag flying over the fort while searching for a place to land. The twins could see soldiers in khaki uniforms running around the parade ground and pointing into the sky. A wide, open field beckoned, and the airplane glided to a smooth landing and rolled to a stop less than thirty feet from the main gate. Before they could release their seat belts, they were surrounded by a small army of soldiers.

A man who looked to be an officer stepped up to the children. "My gosh," he muttered. "Young kids in an old airplane. How did you come to be here?"

When Lacey began to blurt out her story, the officer held up a hand to quiet her. "Come with me," he said in a kindly manner. "I'll take you to my commanding officer, Colonel Rumby."

The colonel was a gray-haired man with one eye brown and the other gray. The gray one looked out to the side and was very distracting.

Both children told of the people of Gold City being held prisoner and forced to work in the mines. To their surprise, kindly Colonel Rumby believed their story from the first word to the last. He looked up at his younger officer. "That explains why nobody in Gold City answers their telephone." He came to his feet. "Captain Crowsfeet, assemble the troop. We're riding to Gold City at full gallop." The colonel turned to Lacey and Casey. "I'd like you to fly above us and keep a sharp eye out for the Boss and his henchmen, should they try to escape."

"Yes sir," Casey agreed.

It wasn't long before a troop of fifty men of the U.S. Cavalry, riding on big brown and black horses, charged out of Fort Blodgett and across the desert toward Gold City. Before getting back on board *Vin Fiz,* Casey looked in her fuel tank, thinking they must be almost out of gas, but astoundingly it was full to the brim. An enchanted airplane, he thought, must not need fuel to fly. The twins jumped into the plane and were soon in the air, following the dust cloud that billowed behind the cavalry.

Lacey and Casey reached the hill and looked down at the entrance to the cavern. Women were emptying an ore cart and did not look up. Nor did their henchman guard because *Vin Fiz* was flying as silently as a ghost and looked like a big hawk circling in the sky.

Only when the cavalry troop came charging up the hill, with Colonel Rumby whirling his saber in the air, did Casey tell *Vin Fiz* to land. "Hurry!" Lacey said to Casey. "We have to save Floopy before the Boss harms him."

They leaped from the plane and ran into the mine shaft ahead of the troops. They ran past the ore cart, past the ladies pushing it, past the henchman prodding them along who shouted at them to stop. They broke all records in their mad dash to rescue their dog. Following on their heels came the cavalry troops, who had dismounted their horses, captured the henchman and come bounding into the mine shaft after Lacey and Casey.

Quickly things began to happen. In less time than it takes to say "dingle, fingle, gingle," the troops had rounded up the rest of the henchmen, stood them against a wall with their hands in the air and trapped the Boss in his cavern bedroom. "You'll never take me alive," said he.

"Then we'll use dynamite to bury you under a ton of rock," Colonel Rumby threatened him.

"Please, Colonel," Lacey begged. "Our beloved dog is in there."

Before the words were out of her mouth, a great yowl came from the Boss as he bellowed in pain. Suddenly, he burst out of his bedroom and ran into the mine shaft with Floopy's jaws firmly dug into his behind. At the sight of Lacey and Casey, Floopy let loose of the Boss and ran over to the twins, wildly wagging his long, slender tail. He licked their faces and barked with joy as the Boss, still rubbing his pants where Floopy had bit him, was led away by the cavalrymen.

Well, you can imagine the jubilation as the good friends and neighbors of Gold City found themselves free to go to their homes and resume their happy lives. Joyous, they cheered madly and raised Lacey, Casey and Colonel Rumby on their shoulders as they marched, singing at the top of their lungs. The troopers joined in, shouting hooray as they escorted the Boss and his henchmen with their rifles to the town jail, where they promptly locked them up.

Later, at a gala fiesta, everybody danced around *Vin Fiz,* whose yellow and green wings seemed to blush as if she were bashful. Mayor Firepit gave Lacey and Casey a big wooden key painted gold that represented the Key to the City. "From now on," stated Mayor Firepit solemnly, "every year on this day, Gold

City will have a celebration called *Vin Fiz* Day to honor the rescue of the townspeople from the nasty and evil Mr. Boss."

When asked if they would like a share of the gold the townspeople had been forced to dig, Lacey, with Casey's nodding approval, said, "Please use our share of the gold to build a new schoolhouse, church, city hall and town jail."

A mighty cheer went up from all at hearing such generous words.

Early the next morning, it was time to leave and there were fond, affectionate farewells as the twins, along with Floopy, climbed into *Vin Fiz*. Casey checked to see that the bottle containing the grape soda *Vin Fiz* was named after was still tied to the wing strut. The bottle was safely snug, having been unseen and untouched by the Boss and his henchmen. The twins then lifted Floopy into his box and slipped the helmet over his head and long, dangling ears. They climbed into their seats and adjusted their seat belts.

The engine sputtered to life entirely on its own and the airplane rolled down the street, the spin of her propellers leaving behind a cloud of dust. Soon they were free of the ground and circling the town, waving to those below, who cheered and waggled their hands in the air.

Lacey took her diary from her pocket and began recording the day's events. Ahead, the morning sun was creeping over the desert horizon. At Casey's instructions, *Vin Fiz* turned her tail to the fair town of Gold City and its good citizens and set a course toward the east.

Captain Otis Shagnasty, master and owner of the steamboat Muddy Queen, *saw the glider and grabbed it before it could pass over the deck and land in the river.*

7

Across the
Great Mississippi River

The desert soon fell behind, and *Vin Fiz* took them over the lofty, snowcapped Rocky Mountains. The jagged, icy peaks looked like upside-down icicles. The air was chilly that high in the sky, and they all had goose bumps until they reached where the mountains fell away into foothills. Now the airplane flew low again as she carried Casey, Lacey and Floopy out over the Western Plains. The land became flat as far as their eyes could see. For a long time they saw almost no trees except those growing beside dry streambeds and farms separated by miles and miles of dry land. They were thankful when *Vin Fiz* sailed over the lush green countryside bordering fields of golden wheat.

The sky was a glorious peacock blue above, and the wind that rushed past the wings was warm with a heavy trace of humidity. They passed over farms and waved to the startled men working the fields and the women sitting out on porches shelling peas.

"Where do you think we are?" asked Casey.

Lacey consulted her map. "Somewhere over Kansas, I think."

"That's where Dorothy of *The Wizard of Oz* was from."

"And don't forget Toto," said Lacey, laughing as she turned and petted Floopy, whose tongue was hanging out the side of his jaw.

They floated over rolling hills and the picturesque farms of Missouri. It would be dark soon, and Casey began looking for a place to spend the night. The orange ball of the sun was just touching the edge of their world when they found themselves flying over the mighty Mississippi River. A huge white steamboat with a big red paddle wheel on its stern was approaching a bend as its steam whistle gave off a loud shriek. The paddle wheel spun and beat the water into white foam; the tall, twin smokestacks spewed black smoke into the twilight sky.

Without waiting to be asked, *Vin Fiz* dove and spiraled down until she was flying around the steamboat only twenty feet above the surface of the river. She flew around in circles and waggled her wings as if she were trying to say something, perhaps give a warning. But even an enchanted airplane can't talk, and Lacey and Casey had no idea what *Vin Fiz* was trying to tell them.

As the airplane circled the boat, the children could plainly see the big red light on the starboard side of the boat (that would be the right side when facing the bow, which is the front of the boat) and the green light on the port (which means the left side when facing the bow). The captain, who stood with his hands on the big steering wheel in the wheelhouse, and the passengers who were walking the decks stared in wonder at the funny-looking aircraft flown by two young children and a dog as it circled the boat.

Abruptly, to the surprise of the twins, *Vin Fiz* leveled off and zoomed upriver and around the bend. Once on the other side and out of sight of the steamboat, Lacey and Casey were shocked to see an immense coal barge, carried by the swift current, drifting wildly down the center of the river. It was black and menacing. From the air they could see that it would soon hurtle around the bend, directly into the path of the unsuspecting captain of the riverboat, who could not see the danger. The looming collision seemed unavoidable.

Far behind the barge came a towboat, whistle blowing, propellers thrashing as the engines ran at full speed in chase of the runaway barge. (If you've wondered how towboats got their name since they almost always push barges instead of pulling them, it is because when barges are tied together they are called a *tow*, hence a towboat moves them.)

"We've got to warn the captain of the steamboat," cried Lacey.

"Quickly!" shouted Casey. "Use a page out of your diary to write a warning."

"How will we drop it to them? The paper will simply blow into the river."

"Not if you fold it into a glider."

As soon as Lacey had finished writing the note, she folded it into a glider with a pointy tail and wide wings.

"Hurry, hurry," Casey shouted at her. "The barge will be coming around the bend any minute."

Realizing the terrible disaster should the barge crash into the steamboat with all its passengers, Casey pleaded with the airplane. "Take us right over the steamboat, *Vin Fiz,* quickly."

With no hesitation, the ungainly craft turned back around the bend and swooped low over the steamboat. Lower and lower she swooped around the towering black smokestacks. At the exact moment they passed over the wheelhouse, Lacey threw the glider and motioned to the captain, who was standing outside the wheelhouse gazing at the antics of *Vin Fiz.*

Captain Otis Shagnasty, master and owner of the steamboat *Muddy Queen,* saw the glider and grabbed it before it could pass over the deck and land in the river.

Uncertainty crossed his mind for a moment. Airplanes rarely dropped notes on riverboats warning them of danger, and this was an especially strange-looking airplane. But Captain Shagnasty had almost two hundred passengers and thirty crew members to consider. A man with a body bent like an S, he tugged at his long spiral mustache, straightened his cap and whistled shrilly into the speaking tube that ran from the wheelhouse to the boiler room.

His chief engineer, Hiram Gooberdum, yelled back, "What is it, Captain?"

"I've just received a warning there's a runaway barge bearing down on us upriver." The captain didn't tell Gooberdum how he knew because he thought the chief engineer might laugh at him. "Reverse engines. Full speed astern."

"Aye, aye," answered Gooberdum as he grabbed the big brass lever that changed the gears for the stern wheel. First he pulled it into neutral, waited a moment and then threw the lever into reverse, turning and watching the big stern wheel as it pounded the water with its paddle boards, causing water to splash and spray over the stern decks and the passengers who happened to be standing there.

At that moment, Captain Shagnasty saw the barge. Pushed by the river current, it surged directly toward the *Muddy Queen.* The barge was huge, loaded with coal and as menacing as any horrible monster. And it was coming as if steered by an evil hand.

Lacey and Casey could only look on helplessly as the gap between the two vessels narrowed. The *Muddy Queen* was picking up speed in reverse, but could she move fast enough to evade the immense black barge? The towboat came pounding around the bend, but it would arrive too late. To Lacey and Casey it did not seem like the steamboat could escape disaster. Closer and closer and closer came the barge. All looked lost. They saw that the steamboat could not get away in time and all her passengers and crew seemed doomed.

But suddenly, *Vin Fiz* took matters into her own hands, or should we say wingtips, and dove toward the water. The airplane slowed and hovered over the big black barge. Then she gently descended until her wheels and runners met the pile of coal and she settled in. With her wheels firmly embedded in the coal, *Vin Fiz* raced her engine until each of her propellers spun and blurred, turning faster than the eye could follow. A great gust of wind blasted past her tail, and Lacey and Casey knew what their airplane was trying to do. She was using all her power to brake the barge's speed down the river.

For more than two agonizing minutes, nothing happened. Then slowly, very slowly, the barge began to slow down. The change was barely noticeable at first, but the speed finally slackened and the gap between the barge and the steamboat started to widen. Now the towboat could reach the barge in time to prevent a collision. A crewman threw over a rope, and together Lacey and Casey jumped from *Vin Fiz* and huffed and puffed as they lifted the heavy rope over a bollard, which is a metal post used to fasten towing and mooring lines. (A *line,* by the way, is nautical talk for rope.) The towboat captain then eased his throttles into reverse and stopped the barge dead in the water.

Safely back in their seats with safety belts fastened, the twins sat back as *Vin Fiz* lifted majestically into the air again and made a circuit around the *Muddy Queen.* A rousing cheer went up from the passengers of the steamboat that echoed up and down the river. Captain Shagnasty loudly rang the boat's bell while yanking furiously on the steam whistle cord. The barge captain also tooted his air horn, adding to the din. One final circle, and at Casey's command *Vin Fiz* flew over the east bank of the Mississippi and resumed her course, heading toward darkening skies.

"I'm getting hungry," said Lacey. "Why don't we find a place to eat and sleep for the night?"

"You're always hungry," Casey muttered, having resigned himself to the whims of girls. He motioned into the fading light at a harvested field beside a group of farm buildings. "Maybe the people who live there can put us up for the night. Mother and Father never turn away people who seek food and shelter."

Hearing this, *Vin Fiz* dipped toward the farm and set her wheels down in the yard beside the house just as the sun faded and disappeared over a grove of trees. Casey lifted Floopy from his box to the ground. Happy to be free again, the basset hound ran in circles and barked with delight. The farmer's dog, hearing the commotion, came running from the house and howled at the intruders. It was a big brown and white dog of no particular breed, friendly, with a shaggy tail that wagged like a flag in a strong breeze. The dogs touched noses and danced around each other, happy to see one of their own kind. As the twins neared the front of the house, the farmer came out and approached.

"Well, well," he boomed good-naturedly. "What have we here?"

"We were passing over," explained Casey, "and wondered if we might trouble you for a meal and bed for the night. I can pay you two dollars." Being a thrifty lad, Casey did not mention that he still had two dollars in his pocket, one having been left at the café in Gold City.

"Nonsense," boomed the farmer, who had short, curly red hair and a matching beard. "You two tykes can stay as long as you like as my guests. My name is Craven Cranberry. Me and old Abercrombe here," he said, scratching his dog behind the ears, "we live alone. We'd enjoy having company. I made meat loaf. I hope you like meat loaf."

"We love meat loaf," said Lacey. "Our mother makes a wonderful meat loaf."

He gazed at *Vin Fiz*. "Did you fly here in that . . . that thing?"

"All the way from California," answered Casey, staying clear of saying Castroville, since no one seemed to know where it was.

"By golly, that's a long way. Now come along, wash up and we'll sit right down at the table."

The twins enjoyed a delicious dinner with Mr. Cranberry, who amused them with stories of his life of adventuring around the world before he settled down on his farm in southern Illinois. Not wanting to keep his young guests up late, Mr. Cranberry showed them up to their bedrooms at nine o'clock. "Sleep tight," he said with a big smile, "and I'll see you in the morning."

The twins were soon fast asleep and quickly went into dreamland, wondering in their dreams if their mother and father had missed them. They were still sound asleep when the farm rooster began crowing *cock-a-doodle-doo* and woke them up.

After a hearty breakfast, Lacey and Casey showed Mr. Cranberry their airplane. The kindly old gentleman had fixed them a box lunch of cold meat loaf sandwiches, which they put in Floopy's box. He pointed at Lacey's map, which she had laid out on the ground, tracking a line across Illinois into Indiana.

"All you have to do from now on is follow the railroad tracks to the east. They should take you straight into New York."

After saying their good-byes, *Vin Fiz* started the engine herself and the children were quickly airborne, waving to Mr. Cranberry and Abercrombe as they became smaller and smaller until they finally disappeared.

Without being told, *Vin Fiz* soon found the railroad tracks and turned east toward the rising sun.

*The silver rails flashed below in a blur
that dazzled their eyes.*

8

The Runaway Train

The state of Indiana came and went. They flew around the famous Indianapolis racetrack where racing cars hurtled over the great oval on Memorial Day. But on this day, the track and the spectator stands were empty. Then it was into Ohio, and they flew merrily over a tapestry of green, rolling hills of thick, leafy woodlands and meadows filled with rainbow-colored flowers.

"Where are we?" Casey asked for the umpteenth time.

"The city off to the right is Chillicothe," Lacey replied after consulting her map.

"That's a funny name."

Unerringly, *Vin Fiz* followed the shiny twin rails of the railroad track. They found it interesting how the rails came together as they vanished miles ahead over the horizon. Pretty soon, they spotted a train stopped on the tracks.

Casey immediately sensed something was not right. "That's odd," he said.

"What's odd?" asked Lacey.

"That train we're approaching. It's stopped."

"So, why is that odd?"

"That's a passenger train. It only stops at a station when it comes into town. There is no town, and there is no station. It's sitting in the middle of the countryside."

"Maybe it broke down."

"Let's fly over and take a look."

Vin Fiz immediately zoomed lower until she was flying only ten feet above the tracks as she sped toward the last car of the train. For an instant it looked as though she was going to crash into the rear car, but with just fifty feet to go, she lifted and flew over the railcars with her wheels almost touching the tops of the roofs. Rushing over the five passenger cars, a dining car, a baggage car, the coal tender and finally the big steam locomotive, painted blue with gold, the twins took a close look at what was happening.

What was happening, they quickly realized, was that the train had not broken down but had been stopped by a gang of bandits, who were looting the passengers of their valuables and removing whatever money and gold that was being shipped in the baggage car. After robbing the passengers alongside the track, the bandits had forced them back into the railroad cars. Alongside the locomotive, not far from the track, the engineer and fireman had been tied to a tree.

All this Lacey and Casey took in at the blink of an eye . . . well, maybe ten blinks. They had hardly passed through the smoke rising from the locomotive's tall smokestack when they heard loud bangs and strange whizzing noises. Floopy started barking and wiggling around in his box as if trying to tell the twins something. *Vin Fiz* instantly knew what was happening because holes suddenly appeared in her wings.

"Oh my gosh!" Lacey cried. "The bandits are shooting at us."

No sooner said than *Vin Fiz* turned sharply and flew behind a grove of tall oak trees, becoming lost to the bandits' sight. The airplane's engine roared and then sputtered before roaring again as if she was expressing her anger.

"We've got to do something!" Casey said urgently.

"We must fly to the nearest town and tell the police chief," Lacey replied.

"Little country towns have sheriffs, not police chiefs."

"What difference does it make as long as they are the law?"

There was no more talk. It was time for action. Casey saw a farmhouse by a lake and said, "There, *Vin Fiz*, land near the house."

Before you could say "dingle, fingle, gingle," the airplane's wheels touched down and rolled to a stop at the front door of the farmhouse. In a flash, Lacey was pounding on the door. It was thrown open by a big, round woman wearing a green apron and holding a bowl with an egg beater.

"My good gracious, children, what's all the commotion?" Then she saw the airplane with a basset hound wearing a leather helmet and goggles staring at her, his huge tongue folded down from between his teeth. "What in the world . . ." She stared at them, confused. "Where on earth did you come from?"

Before Casey could stop her, Lacey said, "Castroville, California."

"Land sakes, I know Castroville. That's where artichokes come from."

Casey was dumbfounded. He couldn't believe they had finally found someone who knew Castroville.

"Please," Lacey implored, "you must call the sheriff and tell him a train is being robbed no more than a mile from your farm."

The big pear-shaped farm lady was not sure she believed Lacey. She looked down at her with a surprised expression and asked, "The train is being robbed?"

Lacey nodded. "It has been stopped by bandits who are robbing the passengers. Call your local sheriff quickly. There might still be time to catch them before they get away."

The woman, disbelief in her eyes, studied Lacey and saw that the little girl was close to tears. "All right. I'll call Sheriff Mugwump and tell him the train has been held up by robbers." Like an elephant leading a stampede, the enormous farm lady turned and hurried inside to the telephone.

"Hurry," Casey yelled to Lacey. "We've got to return so we can follow the robbers and see where they go."

What they saw when *Vin Fiz* flew around the train again, while keeping out of range of the bandits' guns, sent cold shivers up their necks. The bandits were piling their loot in the back of a green bus in preparation for their getaway. Casey counted five of them, all with masks and stocking caps pulled low to conceal the color of their hair. Two of them shot their pistols at *Vin Fiz* as she came in closer to the scene. That was scary enough, but what was even scarier was that the bandits had engaged the throttle of the train, which had begun moving down the track. This might have been a good thing if the engineer and fireman had been in the locomotive's cab. But they were still tied to the tree. With no one operating the valves and levers in the cab, the entire train quickly increased speed and became a runaway with more than a hundred men, women and children trapped helplessly inside the passenger cars.

"We must do something to save all those poor people," Lacey said loudly over the rush of the wind.

"No way we can stop the train," said Casey, looking out the corner of one eye to see what direction the bandits were escaping.

"We can't just fly around and do nothing."

"At least we can fly ahead of the train and warn any other trains that might be on the same track. We can do that much." Then he gripped the control levers, not so much to steer the airplane as to feel the pluck and spirit of *Vin Fiz* through his fingertips. "Go!" he urged the enchanted airplane. "Fly as fast as you can over the track ahead of the train."

Vin Fiz needed no urging. As if she could understand Casey's every word, she made a wide turn and began skimming down the tracks at a speed that took the twins' breath away. Faster and faster the Wright biplane flew. The silver rails flashed below in a blur that dazzled their eyes. They looked so close, it seemed that Lacey could reach down and touch them—not that she actually thought of trying.

The telephone lines along the track hurtled by faster than Casey could count them. The twins had never realized *Vin Fiz* could plunge through the air so fast, so fast that they were pressed back against their seats, unable to lean forward. They could do nothing but clutch the armrests of their seats as fields of corn and wheat swept past with alarming speed.

The airplane had no speedometer or air speed indicator, so they had no idea how fast they were flying, but they would have bet every penny in their piggy banks that they were going a hundred miles an hour.

Floopy was in dog heaven. Like a dog in a car leaning out an open window smelling the dozens of strange scents carried on the breeze, he sniffed and sniffed and sniffed. A basset hound's nose is very sensitive, and he soaked in the aromas from the surrounding countryside in a state of bliss.

They spotted two men up ahead pushing the levers of a go-devil up and down. A go-devil, you might like to know, is a handcar used on a railroad for transporting supplies and workers. It looks like a teeter-totter on a table. "Stop!" Casey burst out, and *Vin Fiz* abruptly slowed to a crawl. "Get off the tracks!" Casey yelled at the startled workers. "There is a runaway train coming down the track."

The railroad workmen looked confused for a moment but took Casey at his word, lifted the go-devil off the track and set it out of the way. Then *Vin Fiz* resumed flying over the track as if she were being chased by a giant airplane eater.

All of a sudden, a tunnel appeared ahead. *Vin Fiz* hesitated a few seconds before making her decision. Instead of flying up and over the big hill like any other logical thinking airplane, she frightened the wits out of the twins by flying right into the yawning mouth of the entrance. It was as black as the soot on their fireplace back home. All they could see was a pinprick of light far off in the distance. But *Vin Fiz* flew as straight as an arrow without touching the walls or ceiling of the tunnel until she burst into the sunlight again.

Their fears having flown away, Lacey and Casey were pleasantly surprised to see a small town rising up before them with a train station sitting beside the railroad. But that wasn't all. There beside the station, stopped, was a passenger train filled with people, a train facing in the direction of the approaching runaway locomotive.

The children stared in dismay because they could see that an awful calamity was in the making.

If the train, which was already huffing and puffing in front of the station, could not get out of the way in time, there would be a terrible pileup. Without losing a minute's worth of time, and beyond the twins' understanding, *Vin Fiz* dove toward the railroad track, leveled out in the nick of time and landed in front of the locomotive, coming to a stop a few inches in front of the cowcatcher, a funny-looking, sloping device mounted on the front of the locomotive to push unwanted snags off the tracks. Since cows were always behind fences and almost never walked on the railroad tracks, they rarely had the opportunity to be pushed out of the way by a locomotive's cowcatcher.

Casey and Lacey never argued, never questioned, nor ever doubted the airplane's enchanted wisdom. They ran up to the engineer, the conductor and the stationmaster, who were standing on the loading platform, and breathlessly told the story of the bandits and the runaway train.

The engineer and conductor did not doubt, or wonder if the children were telling a story. All they asked was if the train was approaching on the same track. When told it was, they stared at each other in alarm.

The conductor, in his black uniform and round cap, scratched his chin. "How odd," he said slowly.

"The *Sunrise Express* should be on the north-south track, not the east-west. Let's wire the station at the junction and see if it passed by."

Everyone rushed into the station, where the conductor ordered the man who operated the telegraph to wire the station up the line and ask if the *Sunrise Express* had passed by. The answer came back in seconds. No, the *Sunrise Express* had not passed. It was more than thirty minutes late.

"That can mean only one thing," the stationmaster said with alarm. "The bandits must have switched the *Sunrise Express* onto the wrong track. That's why, as the children have reported, it's headed in this direction."

"The *Sunrise Express* is pulled by a Super Morpheus 4-6-2," said the engineer. "She's the fastest engine on the line."

"A 4-6-2?" asked Casey, always fascinated by anything mechanical.

The engineer smiled. "That refers to the engine's wheels," he explained. "Four small ones up front, six drive wheels, and two small wheels in the rear, 4-6-2."

"Not good," said the conductor. "A Super Morpheus can run a hundred and twenty miles an hour. Our train, the *Moonlight Limited*, is much slower."

The engineer looked troubled indeed. "The nearest siding where we can pull off the main track is twelve miles away. We could never reach it in time. Not before colliding with the *Sunrise Express* if its throttle is set on full steam and with no hand on the brake."

"That's only if she makes it around Eternity Curve," said the conductor. "If the *Sunrise Express* is running at full throttle, she'll jump the tracks for sure before she reaches our train."

"We had better get everyone off the *Moonlight Limited*," said the stationmaster. "You haven't a moment to lose to back safely out of the way."

The conductor emptied the passenger cars in no time and waved his hand at the engineer, who was already in the cab waiting for the signal. He released the brakes, pushed the reverse lever to the full forward notch, opened the throttle and released the sand valves to drop sand between the drive wheels and the rails for more traction, things a steam locomotive engineer has to do to move the train. Then, with a great shower of steam and smoke, the locomotive began backing away from the station. Only the engineer and his fireman remained on the *Moonlight Limited*, ready to jump clear when the *Sunrise Express* came into view, providing she made it around Eternity Curve.

Lacey and Casey were standing there not knowing what to do as the train started to back away from them. They heard a strange sound behind them and turned to see that *Vin Fiz* was bouncing up and down on her wheels and shaking her wings.

"What is she doing?" Lacey wondered aloud.

"I think she's trying to tell us something," said Casey.

Lacey stared at the airplane's antics and suddenly she knew. "She wants us to get on board."

The twins leaped into their seats. As quickly as they tightened their seat belts, *Vin Fiz* lifted into the air.

The airplane made a wide half circle and soared over the tracks, going back the way she had come. Back through the tunnel, back through the corn and wheat fields, back past the telegraph poles. Her engine racing so fast it whirred and hummed, *Vin Fiz* devoured the miles in her dash toward the runaway train. Faster than the wind, faster than the birds, faster than the clouds scooting across the bright blue sky, she flew like a flash of light. If there had been a speed record, she would have broken it. As if she was a fox sniffing the wind, *Vin Fiz* pulled up until she was flying five hundred feet above the twin steel tracks. At that height the twins soon saw a wisp of black smoke far up the rails ahead.

"There it is!" Lacey shouted. "There's the *Sunrise Express*. And she's coming like a herd of mad buffaloes!"

"Floopy, go get 'em!"

9

Floopy Leads the Way

And sure as the sun sets in the west, the *Sunrise Express*, with its steam locomotive spouting a thick column of black smoke from its tall smokestack, steam spurting from the sides and its big drive wheels turning faster than the eye could follow, came roaring down the track like some mechanical monster run amok.

When it rounded a long, wide curve, the passenger cars rocked back and forth and came within a cat's whisker of flying off the track. What would happen when it came to Eternity Curve, the sharp bend in the railroad track that ran along a deep canyon?

As the twins soared past the five passenger cars, the dining car and the baggage car, they could see the terrified passengers staring back at them through the windows, their eyes wide with fright. They gestured wildly at the twins as if there was something they could do to stop the train, but short of warning the *Moonlight Limited* at the station, Lacey and Casey were helpless. It was only a matter of minutes before the *Sunrise Express* and all the men, women and children inside would either collide with the other train or shoot off the rails.

"Is there nothing we can do?" moaned Lacey.

Before Casey could answer, *Vin Fiz*, again acting on her own, dipped downward and flew alongside the speeding train until she pulled even with the coal tender. "*Vin Fiz*," Casey shouted at the airplane, "what are you doing?"

But *Vin Fiz* did not answer. Not too surprising when you consider that airplanes can't talk, at least not like we do. She stayed beside the coal tender and eased closer and closer until she slipped over the top and hung there with the smoke streaming back and covering them all with soot. Then she dropped down until her wheels sank into the coal with a soft *ka-thunk*.

"What could *Vin Fiz* be up to?" Lacey wondered excitedly.

Casey was as lost as Lacey. "I can't believe she put us on the runaway train."

The twins well knew by now that *Vin Fiz* rarely did anything without a good reason. It soon dawned on them why the aircraft had set them atop the coal tender. "She wants us to stop the train," said Lacey.

"I agree, but what can we do to stop this thing?" replied Casey. "I've never read a manual on how to operate a locomotive."

"We've got to try. If we try, we can do. If we do, we can achieve and succeed."

Casey was not as optimistic as his sister. He had no doubt that it was up to him. His sister was wiser than he in many subjects, but he was smarter when it came to mechanical devices. It was obvious that *Vin Fiz* had put them on the coal tender so they could make their way to the locomotive's cab. As soon as they loosened their seat belts, they had to hang on for dear life because the speeding train was

115

shaking and rattling violently. The noise of the drive wheels rolling over the rails, the fire in the firebox, the steam escaping out of the cylinders and the wind sweeping over the train was deafening.

Helping Lacey by keeping a protective arm around her, Casey crawled on his hands and knees over the black coal that was used to fuel the boiler of the locomotive. They finally reached the edge and tumbled down the coal pile to the floor of the tender. From there, holding tight to anything they could to keep from being thrown off the twisting and shuddering out-of-control train, they made their way into the engineer's cab.

The first thing that struck them was that the cab was as warm as a desert in summer and hot enough to bake an apple pie. They felt as if they had crawled into an oven. The fiery temperature came from the firebox, the blazing furnace that heated the water in the boiler into steam that powered the engine. The bandits must have shoveled in half a ton of coal before escaping, because the fire was very intense.

The second thing that overwhelmed them was the maze of valves, gauges and levers. There was a steam pressure gauge, a temperature gauge, a water gauge and at least ten valves, all painted red. And there were two long levers, one labeled REVERSE, which rose from the floor of the cab, and the other marked THROTTLE and extending from the top of the firebox.

"Oh no!" shouted Lacey over the clanging and hissing of the mighty engine. "Here comes the station!"

They only had time for a quick glance as the *Sunrise Express* roared past the station like a tornado, nearly blowing the conductor, the stationmaster and the passengers from the other train off the platform. And then the station and all the people were left behind with a big *whoosh,* and the *Sunrise Express* continued on its mad, crazy journey to certain destruction at Eternity Curve.

Casey stood his ground and studied the entanglement of valves and pipes that looked like the thick underbrush of a jungle. "Let's begin by turning the valves off," he said, trying to look as if he knew what he was doing.

"Which ones?" asked Lacey.

"Take your pick. I'll take the levers."

The valve handles were hot to the touch, but Lacey found a glove left behind by the abducted fireman and began spinning the handles as fast as she could. She knew that to close a valve, you had to turn it to the right. She remembered the words "lefty loosely, rightly tightly." At first nothing happened, but as she closed the fourth valve, a round one bigger than the others, she got lucky. Lacey had cut off the steam to the great pistons that plunged back and forth inside the cylinders that moved the drive wheels. "I think she's slowing," she burst happily.

"You did it!" Casey shouted. "She's definitely slowing."

Indeed, the train had slowed but not nearly enough. Lacey had stopped the power that drove the train, but its momentum kept it barreling over the tracks like a rocket ship.

Eternity Curve had come into sight, and so did the *Moonlight Limited*, which was just backing through the sharp turn, doing its best to switch tracks before the *Sunrise Express* crashed into it.

While Lacey was frantically twisting the valves, Casey had spent the time studying the labels on the various levers. He pulled the lever that was labeled BRAKES from the "off" to the "on" position.

"Hooray!" he shouted as the air brakes took hold on all the passenger cars and their steel wheels began skidding over the tracks.

It still wasn't enough to stop the runaway train. Though its speed was down to ninety miles an hour, that meant it was traveling at 132 feet a second—and it was only two hundred yards away from charging around Eternity Curve at a speed fast enough to jump the tracks. Casey then pulled the lever marked REVERSE to its full stop. The big drive wheels instantly reversed their whirl forward and began spinning in the opposite direction. But with steel wheels against steel rails, there was almost no grip between them, and the wheels merely skidded over the rails.

Eternity Curve was barely fifty yards away, and the other train only another fifty yards farther.

But Casey wasn't finished.

The throttle was already full open, with the engine running in reverse. As fast as his hands could move, he opened the two valves that were tagged SAND VALVES. Sand flowed onto the tracks beneath the drive wheels, giving them traction. Now able to grip the rails, the great steel wheels gained a firm hold and assisted the brakes in stopping the train.

The train was entering Eternity Curve down from ninety miles an hour to fifty, still a dangerous speed for such a sharp turn. Meanwhile, the *Moonlight Limited* was backing at forty miles an hour, and the *Sunrise Express* was gaining on it.

Whipping into the sharp curve, the speeding train and all its cars leaned sideways, the outer wheels lifting off the rail. Yet, dragged by the brakes and the drive wheels that were forcing it backward, the train clung to the track like an owl on a tree limb.

For a few seconds it was touch and go, but finally, to the great relief of Lacey, Casey, the engineer and fireman in the cab of the *Moonlight Limited*'s engine and all the passengers on the *Sunrise Express*, the train ground to a stop, a great puff of black smoke rising through its smokestack with a billowing hiss of steam.

Oh, the excitement, the adventure, the danger and the thrill! Thankfully, it was all over.

But not quite.

Before they could be thanked by the engineer, fireman and all the passengers of the *Sunrise Express* for saving their lives, Lacey and Casey turned their sights on catching the bandits who had caused such a great calamity. Once more they rose into the sky, with *Vin Fiz* lifting them straight up from the coal tender and turning back to where they had last seen the despicable bandits. Now the trick was to pick up the trail the bandits had left during their getaway. Was *Vin Fiz* up to the chase? the twins wondered. Could she track a cold trail to the bandits' hideout?

The twins didn't have long to wait.

As they flew over the spot where the *Sunrise Express* was robbed, they could see four cars marked Oglebee County Sheriff's Department. Sheriff Mugwump and his deputies were talking to the engineer and fireman from the *Sunrise Express*, who had been untied from the tree. They flew on until they came to a crossroad. Then Casey told *Vin Fiz* to land, and she did.

The enchanted airplane wasn't the only one who could track a human trail. As soon as the wheels rolled to a halt, Casey lifted Floopy to the ground and said, "Floopy, go get 'em!"

Floopy instantly barked up a storm and began running down the road that led west. Knowing they could never keep up with Floopy on foot, the twins jumped back in the airplane, which lifted off and followed the basset hound from a hundred feet in the air. They studied the surrounding countryside, looking for a green bus. At every crossroad, Floopy stopped and sniffed the air with his supersensitive black nose. Catching the scent of the bandits, he rushed down a road leading to the north. A mile later, he stopped at a junction where a small dirt road angled into a forest. He circled with his nose to the ground, then, satisfied, picked the correct scent and chased off over a road that was overgrown with weeds.

Lacey, Casey and *Vin Fiz* followed from the air but saw only a thick blanket of leaves after Floopy disappeared under the trees. *Vin Fiz* quieted her engine so it ran silently with no popping from the exhaust pipes. Only she knew how, and she did it. Now for the second time, Lacey and Casey felt like they were in a glider soaring soundlessly with the breeze.

They flew over a field of weeds that had once been filled with crops. It looked to have been long abandoned and had returned to nature. In the middle of the field was a deserted mansion. Not an ordinary house, mind you, but a country manor built of stone and almost as large as a castle. It must have belonged to a local landowner whose family moved away long ago.

There was a gatehouse with a high archway that led to a central courtyard. The main three-story building was arranged around the courtyard with smaller outer buildings for the stables and quarters for the servants. But they all looked deserted and run-down, not having been maintained in many years. Spires rose everywhere, joined by at least eight tall chimneys. Four round towers with cone-shaped roofs stood on the four corners of the manor.

Lacey thought it looked spooky and haunted. She could almost imagine the clip-clop of ghostly horses in the courtyard. The manor stood partially ruined, a sad shadow of its former glory.

Floopy sat in front of the big rusty gate to the courtyard, happily wagging his tail at knowing he had traced the bandits to their hideout.

"After we land, you and *Vin Fiz* fly back and tell the sheriff we've found where the bandits are hiding," Casey told Lacey. "I'll scout around and see what I can find."

"I don't see the green bus," Lacey protested.

"They must have hidden it."

"How can you be sure?"

"Floopy wouldn't have led us here if he hadn't followed the scent of the bandits."

"You be careful," said Lacey, worried for the safety of her brother.

"Never fear," Casey said bravely.

Understanding Casey's plan, *Vin Fiz* touched down and quickly took off again as Casey leaped to the ground and ran toward the wall before making his way to the big iron gate. It looked to Casey as if the gate had not been opened for a long time because all the bars were very rusty. But then he stared down at the ground and saw the tire tracks of a big truck or bus. He was trying to figure out how to get past the gate, which had a huge lock and chain, when Floopy dropped down on his stomach and wiggled under it. Casey did the same and followed him.

Once in the courtyard, he crept softly without making a sound to the partly open door of what was once the stable for the owner's horses. Casey peeked inside and saw a long red bus. Oh no, he thought. He had hoped to find a green bus. He stepped up to it and pressed one hand against the front fender. The paint was sticky. He scraped off some with a coin from his pocket and saw that the bus was green under the red. The bandits had repainted it so it wouldn't be identified as the getaway vehicle. There was no doubt that this was the bandits' hideout. Now, if only they would stay put until Lacey could return with Sheriff Mugwump and his deputies.

Finding a door that led from the stables to the house, Casey sneaked inside. A long hall trailed down to the great main room of the manor. Pressing his back against the wall, he slinked to the archway above the far door and listened to the voices coming from the great room. He was shocked to hear a voice that sounded amazingly similar to that of the Boss, the very same Boss who had tried to steal all the gold. But it couldn't be. He was in jail in Nevada. Casey peeked around the door and saw five men. His heart skipped a beat when he saw that one of them looked just like the evil Boss in the gold mine.

He was saying, "So here's what we'll do. We take the money from the train robbery and use it to break my brother, the Boss, and his henchmen out of jail in Nevada. Then we join forces on a nationwide crime spree, robbing trains, armored cars and banks. We'll clean up millions of dollars before skipping the country."

"I like that," said a man with a face like a blood-hound.

"Me too," said a man with a face like a ferret.

"Count me in," said a man with a face like a raccoon.

"I'm with you, Chief," said a man with a face like a coyote.

Casey was flabbergasted. He couldn't believe his ears. The Chief was the Boss's brother, and he was the leader of another gang of hoodlums. And the scheming brothers, along with their henchmen and gang, were planning a national crime wave! The mere thought raised the yellow hair on Casey's neck. He turned to flee the manor and tell Sheriff Mugwump, but before he could sneak back down the hall to the stable, Floopy trotted past him into the great room.

Floopy was hungry, and he didn't care who knew it. Humans were humans in his dog mind. Some, like Lacey and Casey and the Nicefolks, were kind to him, and he loved them. But when it came to food, he'd lick any human hand that offered to feed him. He came up to the long table the gang was seated around and sat down on the cold stone floor, his tongue licking his jaws and his tail thumping the ground.

"Where did this dog come from?" demanded the Chief.

"I have no idea," said Bloodhound Face.

"Me either," said Ferret Face.

"Don't look at me," said Raccoon Face.

"I'm in the dark," said Coyote Face.

The Chief picked up Floopy and set him on the table. "I never saw a dog wearing a leather helmet and goggles before. He looks as if he's hungry. Well, that's too bad. Tough luck, dog, we're leaving. Come on, gang, let's take the loot from the train and head for Nevada."

The Chief and his gang turned their backs on Floopy, who stared after them sadly at seeing he wasn't going to be fed.

Casey was filled with dread. There was no sign of the sheriff and his deputies. He began to wonder if Lacey had persuaded them to race to the manor. He couldn't stand there and do nothing. He had to stall the Chief and his gang until Sheriff Mugwump arrived on the scene.

Building his courage, he stepped into the middle of the archway and shouted out in a trembling voice. "Hi there. Have any of you seen my lost dog?"

"First a dog wearing a leather helmet with goggles, and now some kid," the Chief said angrily. Then he studied Casey, and a shrewd look crossed his face. "Hey, I recognize you. Now it comes back to me. You and that dog were on the airplane that flew over us when we were robbing the train. I shot at you."

"Yes," Casey said, acting braver than he felt. "I saw you rob the train, and I want some of the loot or I'll tell Sheriff Mugwump."

"You know the sheriff?" the Chief demanded.

"Well enough."

"So you think you're entitled to a share of our loot." Then he laughed, a long, rolling laugh that echoed throughout the great room. "Ho, ho, that's a good joke, hey, gang?"

"Sure is," said Bloodhound Face.

"You bet," said Ferret Face.

"A riot," said Raccoon Face.

"Real funny," said Coyote Face.

Casey started to say something, but the Chief held up a big red hand. "Silence. Because you had to stick your nose into business that doesn't concern you, that stupid dog and you are coming with us." His expression turned shrewd again. "And along the way you just might have a little unfortunate accident. Right, gang?"

"You bet, Chief," said Bloodhound Face.

"Good idea, Chief," said Ferret Face.

"I'd like that, Chief," said Raccoon Face.

"Sounds good to me, Chief," said Coyote Face.

"That settles it," said the Chief. "Bring them along to the bus." He twisted his face to look menacingly at Casey. "And don't you and that dog try any tricks or you'll both have an accident sooner rather than later."

Casey, now getting desperate because Lacey and Sheriff Mugwump had not arrived, fell down on the floor and clutched his knee. Anything, he thought, to stall another minute. "Oh, my knee, I hurt my knee."

"That's what you get for being clumsy," said the Chief, grabbing him by the arm and dragging him to the stable, where they all climbed into the bus. But not before loading several bags of money that were stolen from the *Sunrise Express* and its passengers.

The Chief sat in the driver's seat and backed the bus into the courtyard, where he turned and steered toward the gatehouse. Then he stopped. Raccoon Face jumped off the bus and slid the key into the lock and unhooked the chain holding the big iron gate closed. As he swung it open, the red bus rolled through and stopped briefly to pick up Raccoon Face. That was as far as the bus moved.

At that moment *Vin Fiz*, with Lacey at the controls, appeared and began circling the big bus.

The Chief looked up through the windshield and blinked. "There's that plane again." He jumped off the bus and raised his pistol to shoot at Lacey and *Vin Fiz*. But before he could blink again and pull the trigger, the Chief found the bus surrounded by Sheriff Mugwump and his deputies, who covered the bandits with an arsenal of shotguns. "Stop right there," ordered the sheriff, "or suffer the consequences."

"What's a consequence?" asked Bloodhound Face.

"Beats me," said Ferret Face.

"I can't rightly say," said Raccoon Face.

"Me either," said Coyote Face.

"It means something we'd be sorry for, you idiots," the Chief grunted. He turned to Casey. "This is all your fault. I should have taken care of you and your stupid dog when I had the chance." At those words, Floopy sank his teeth into the Chief's pant leg and tore his trousers.

"Good thing you'll never get the chance," said Sheriff Mugwump. His deputies shoved the Chief and his gang, protesting and yelling every step of the way, into the sheriff's patrol cars. He turned to Lacey and Casey. "I shouldn't be surprised if there isn't a nice reward from the railroad for your brave conduct today." He leaned down and petted Floopy. "And I'll bet you'll receive a bag of dog bones."

Floopy wagged his tail furiously, wondering when he would be able to sink his teeth into the bones.

"What about *Vin Fiz*?" asked Lacey. "She deserves most of the credit."

Sheriff Mugwump seemed bewildered. "And who, may I ask, is *Vin Fiz*?"

"Our airplane," answered Casey. "We couldn't have done it without her."

The sheriff scratched his chin. "I don't know how you reward an airplane for courage, but I'm sure we'll think of a way." A light seemed to go off in his mind and he smiled. Then he reached up to his shirt and removed his badge. "How about you and your dog and your plane becoming honorary members of the Oglebee County Sheriff's Department?" That said, he pinned the badge on Floopy's leather helmet. *Vin Fiz* trembled her wings with happiness while Floopy's tail thumped the ground.

There were happy good-byes all around, and Sheriff Mugwump promised to have the reward money from the railroad sent to their farm in Castroville.

And then they were in the air once more, flying toward the Northeast and New York. There were white fluffy clouds that dropped a light sheet of rain and made a beautiful rainbow that *Vin Fiz* flew under.

It was a glorious day, and New York was only hours away.

"Grab on!" Casey bellowed. "Now!"

10

Over Niagara Falls

Vin Fiz made a great sweeping turn and flew over the northwest corner of Pennsylvania, hugging the shoreline of Lake Erie. They soared above the water and darted around a fleet of sailboats with white, blue and red sails that were racing across the lake. Puffed by the breeze, the boats skimmed the waves like dancing butterflies. Soon *Vin Fiz* passed over the mouth of a wide river that ran into the lake.

"Where are we now?" asked Casey for the tenth time that morning. "What's that city below?"

Lacey knew without consulting her map. "We're over Buffalo," she said happily. "We've crossed into New York. It won't be long now before we see the Atlantic Ocean."

"*Vin Fiz* should be turning to the east, but she seems intent on flying us north up the river."

"I wonder why," said Lacey.

"What river is it?"

"The Niagara. It's the boundary between the United States and Canada."

They gazed at the wide winding river below whose banks rose up and met lush green fields and forests. Before long, they spotted white mist rising into the sky and heard a huge rumbling sound that became louder and louder until they beheld the awesome beauty and spectacular view of Niagara Falls, where the mighty river fell over cliffs 176 feet high. The Niagara actually split into two rivers. One flowed around Goat Island, forming the American Falls on one side, and the other flowed over Canadian Horseshoe Falls. Almost eight hundred thousand gallons of water rushed over the falls every second.

Lacey and Casey stared in rapture at the river with its surging dark blue water turning into a mixture of white and turquoise as it fell and crashed onto the rocks far below. They could feel the thunder of the falls as the water billowed in a great cloud of white mist.

"Do you think *Vin Fiz* brought us out of the way to see the falls?" Casey shouted above the roar of the water.

"I don't think so," Lacey shouted back. "Look, she's turning and carrying us upriver."

The enchanted airplane had an amazing sense of danger and flew rapidly above the raging water that traveled faster and faster before tumbling over the rocky ledge. Five hundred yards past the falls, Lacey and Casey saw a small rowboat with two teenage girls in it being carried toward the falls. People along the shore were shouting and screaming helplessly as the little boat and its occupants were swept by a thirty-mile-per-hour current toward the boiling brink.

"We must do something to help," cried Lacey, "or they will surely die!"

"*Vin Fiz* will know what to do," yelled back Casey. "See, already she's turning on a course toward the boat."

Vin Fiz knew exactly what to do. The enchanted airplane with the mystical powers somehow sensed there would be a tragedy at Niagara Falls, and only she could prevent it. Lower and lower she came to the water. Closer and closer came the boat to the falls, until only three hundred yards remained.

As *Vin Fiz* slowed and began hovering over the boat, the girls looked up and saw the airplane and the twin pilots. The girls were terrified and clinging to each other; the falls were only two hundred yards away and coming nearer with each passing second. There seemed no way they could be saved from going over the falls.

The airplane began to drop closer to the boat, and Casey saw what *Vin Fiz* was trying to do. He shouted down to the girls, "Grab on to our landing skids and hold tight!"

But the girls were frozen in fright. They made no move to reach up and save themselves.

With less than two hundred yards to go, Casey climbed down from his seat and straddled the landing wheels and skids, reaching out for the girls.

Still they sat huddled in sheer panic.

Now, with only a hundred yards before the thunderous drop-off, *Vin Fiz* took matters into her own hands, or should we say wheels. She dropped until her landing skids were only inches from the girls' upturned faces. Time was running out.

"Grab on!" Casey bellowed. "Now!"

Finally, the girls shook off their terror and reached up. Casey grabbed the wrist of each and yelled again as he saw the water fall into the great churning void not fifty feet ahead. "Clutch the landing skid in your other hand. I can't hold you both."

At last, realizing their horrifying journey over the falls was a mere ten feet away, they seized the skids with their free hands, and not a second too soon. *Vin*

Fiz soared out over the booming roar of the falls as tons of water hurtled beneath the airplane and cascaded onto the rocks far below.

Casey was holding on to the girls with all his might, but he wouldn't be able to keep his grip on their wrists more than another minute. His grip was slipping from the water splashing around him. *Vin Fiz* was well aware of the situation and dove toward the water that crashed into the great mass of rocks in a white cloud of blinding spray.

A boat filled with tourists who had paid to see the falls from the bottom of the gorge appeared out of the mist. Lacey could read the letters on the side of the deck railing. The name of the boat was *Maid of the Mist.*

Without coaxing from Lacey, *Vin Fiz* settled over *Maid of the Mist* and slowly descended until she was hovering ten feet above the main deck. The people on board quickly realized what was happening and reached up toward the two young girls. Seeing that helping hands were less than a foot away from their feet, Casey said, "You can let go, girls. You're safe now."

They released their grip on the wheel skids at the same time that Casey released their wrists. Both girls fell safely into the waiting arms of the boat's passengers. As Casey climbed back into his seat, the girls shouted, "Thank you, oh, thank you!" The passengers waved and applauded along with all the people lining the shore who had witnessed the rescue.

Vin Fiz acted as though she were human, dancing and waggling her wings in the sky. Lacey and Casey marveled at her antics while wondering how an airplane could have such mystical vision. They would never know how she knew those two girls were about to go over the falls.

She and the twins made one more pass over the thunderous cascade before *Vin Fiz* turned her wings toward the Atlantic Ocean and the end of their long journey.

"So much happened, it doesn't seem real."

11

The Fantastic Journey Ends

The sun began to set behind *Vin Fiz*'s tail, and darkness was creeping over the land when Lacey and Casey saw the lights of New York City blinking in the distance. They gazed in awe as the lights sparkled from the windows of the tall buildings that seemed to touch the sky. Looking down and seeing the streets crawling with thousands of cars was a spectacular sight.

Vin Fiz seemed as if she was enjoying the sight too. She swooped playfully around the tops of the buildings, many of which had lush roof gardens.

"Look, Casey," said Lacey excitedly, "there's the Empire State Building."

"I see it," replied Casey. "The big open part of the city is Central Park."

"The lights of Broadway are beneath us."

"And here comes Wall Street."

When *Vin Fiz* reached the tip of Manhattan Island called the Battery, she banked out over the Hudson River and flew past the Statue of Liberty.

"Isn't she beautiful?" gushed Lacey. "I didn't know she was green." She paused to point at several large brick buildings on a nearby island. "What is that?"

"Haven't you seen pictures of Grandpa Nicefolk? When he came from Europe, he had to go through Ellis Island with all the other new people who came here. He took a picture of his first day in America standing in front of the main building under the flag."

It was getting dark now, and the twins began looking for a place to land. Luckily for them, a full moon rose across the heavens. It was so bright, Lacey could read her map.

"There's a nice sandy beach by the seashore. We can land there and spend the night, since it's so comfortable and warm."

"That would be fun," said Casey, "going to sleep looking at the stars and moon while we listen to the waves roll in from the ocean."

"I'd really like that," Lacey said dreamily.

Casey put his hands on the control levers, wishing he could once again control the airplane, which had been flying itself since leaving Castroville. *Vin Fiz* sensed what was on Casey's mind and allowed him to level out before slowly gliding in toward a wide sandy beach. The wheels touched down in the soft sand, and the skids plowed to a stop. The engine went quiet, and the propellers ticked over slowly before finally coming to a rest.

"We've done it, sister," Casey said happily. "We've flown across the great United States."

"With no small help from *Vin Fiz*," Lacey reminded him.

He patted the wing with affection. "True. Without her we'd still be back in Castroville, only dreaming about the places we've seen from the clouds."

"So much happened, it doesn't seem real." Floopy

jumped from his box and ran up and down the beach and around the airplane out of happiness at being on the ground again. He had often accompanied the Nicefolk family on picnics to the beach at Castroville. Being a dog, without the ability to think great thoughts, Floopy thought he was on a Pacific Ocean beach, surely not on one more than three thousand miles away. To him, if you'd seen one beach, you'd seen them all. He lay down on his stomach in the sand and promptly fell asleep.

As the twins lay in the sand and stared up at the moon and stars, Lacey said, "I hope we don't have so many adventures on the flight home. We've already had enough to last us a lifetime."

"Not likely," said Casey. "The trip will probably be boring."

"Do you think Mother and Father are worried?"

"I don't think so. We camped by the river in the forest for three days only a month ago."

"I miss them."

"We'll see them soon," Casey consoled her.

"Look, a shooting star," said Lacey, pointing at a streak through the sky.

"I wonder if we'll ever ride a rocket ship to the stars."

"Maybe Mr. Sucop could make us one."

"A rocket ship to the stars," said Casey, his eyelids beginning to droop. "That might be asking too much."

"We could try, couldn't we?" asked Lacey, letting her lively imagination flow unhindered.

"Yes . . . ," Casey answered, two blinks away from sleep. "We can try. But let's get some sleep first. We'll want to take off early in the morning."

Then, under a moon as bright as a big round beacon and beneath a carpet of stars, the twins drifted off to sleep to the sounds of the waves curling in from far at sea.

"Mercy me!"

12

Home Again

When Lacey woke up the next morning, it wasn't to the sound of the surf but to the sound of the Nicefolk family rooster. She sat up, rubbed her eyes and stared around her.

She was back in her own bed in her own room on the farm.

In a daze and not knowing what to make of going to sleep on a beach in New York and waking up in Castroville, she climbed from her bed and looked out the window. The herb fields still surrounded the family farm. She also gazed thoughtfully at the mystical barn from where she and Casey had left on their journey across country.

Vin Fiz was nowhere to be seen.

Her mind adrift, she walked down the hall to her brother's room, truly believing she had awakened from an exciting and wonderful dream. She found Casey sitting on the side of his bed staring dumbly at his pajamas, wondering when he had put them on.

"We're home," he said, bewildered.

"Of course we're home," she echoed.

He looked at her. "I had the most wonderful dream."

"So did I."

"I dreamed we flew across the United States to New York. On the way, we helped rescue a Western town's citizens from working as slaves in a gold mine and saved a steamboat from being struck by a runaway barge."

"That was before we stopped a runaway train and saved two girls from going over Niagara Falls," Lacey said in growing wonder.

"That was my dream," said Casey, surprised.

"That was my dream too."

Casey shook his head in befuddlement. "How could we both have had the same dream?"

"It all seemed so real," Lacey said wistfully.

"But if it really happened, how did we get home so quickly? I don't remember flying back."

At that moment, Mr. Nicefolk leaned through the doorway and said, "All right, kids, rise and shine. Breakfast is ready. School is out for the summer and you've spent enough time camping in the woods. You've got chores to do."

The twins looked at each other with an expression of puzzlement on their faces.

"He didn't act as if we'd been gone for days," said Lacey.

"How strange," Casey said as he dropped his feet onto the floor.

Ima and Ever Nicefolk ate their breakfast with the

children as if today was like any other day. Nothing was said about their disappearing for such a long time. Even Floopy ate out of his dog bowl as if he'd never left home in an airplane.

Just as they were finishing breakfast, Mr. Nobblebob, the town delivery man, knocked on the screen door. "Come in, come in, Mr. Nobblebob," invited Ever Nicefolk. "What brings you out to our farm?"

"You have a very important letter that you have to sign for," said Mr. Nobblebob, a short man with a shiny bald head, who delivered letters and packages on a motorcycle.

"Can I get you a cup of coffee?" offered Ima Nicefolk.

"No, thank you. I must be on my way. Lots of packages to deliver."

As soon as Mr. Nobblebob left, Ever Nicefolk opened the envelope and a bank check dropped out along with a letter. He put on his reading spectacles, and his face went blank as he read the words written in the letter.

"Mercy, mercy," said Ima Nicefolk. "Don't tease us. Tell us what it says."

Slowly, as if in a dream, Mr. Nicefolk held up the check. "This is a check made out to the Nicefolk family for ten thousand dollars."

"Mercy me," said the astonished Ima Nicefolk. "Who on earth would send us a check for ten thousand dollars?"

"The letter is from Sheriff Mugwump from Oglebee County, Ohio."

Lacey and Casey stared at each other across the table in wide-eyed astonishment, too stunned to speak.

"Well, stop standing there like a dummy and tell us what it says," said Ima impatiently.

"It says the check is from the Ohio and

Chillicothe Railroad as a reward. It doesn't say for what."

Ever Nicefolk slowly shook his head. "There must be some mistake."

"Who is the check made out to?"

Ever held it up to the light. "It's made out to the Nicefolk family of Castroville, California."

"Mercy me!"

"The railroad must have sent the check to the wrong Nicefolk family."

"No mistake," Ima said seriously as she held up the check. "We're the only Nicefolks in and around Castroville."

Lacey and Casey sat silent without saying anything, afraid to tell of their adventures and still not sure if it all hadn't been a dream.

"What we'll do," said Ever finally, "is deposit the check in our account but not spend the money. I'll write the Ohio and Chillicothe Railroad. If they say it's a mistake, we can send it back."

"And if they say there is no mistake and tell us to keep the money?" asked Ima Nicefolk hesitantly.

A wise smile turned up the corners of his mouth. "Then we'll use it to buy that new machine we've always wanted that can automatically package our herbs for market. Then we'll no longer have to do it by hand."

"Oh, that would be wonderful," said Ima Nicefolk happily. "At last we could make the farm profitable."

Lacey and Casey excused themselves and hurried from the kitchen with Floopy running along beside them. "If we didn't dream of saving the train," said Lacey, "and we really did it, Mother and Father will get their machine."

"I still can't believe it happened," said Casey.

"We'll know as soon as we find *Vin Fiz*."

Casey threw open the door to the porch, and the twins rushed outside.

To their dismay, there was no *Vin Fiz*.

"Oh dear," moaned Lacey. "Our big adventure did not happen."

"It must have," said Casey, looking around the farmyard. Then his face lit up. "Wait, maybe she's in the barn."

They ran inside the barn, and Lacey pointed to the magic pad. "Look," she cried. There, sitting small and quiet, was the model of *Vin Fiz* that her brother had built. "She never got big."

Casey was disheartened. "No," he said softly as he picked up the little model, "it looks just the same." Then he held the model to the light and stared at it. Suddenly his eyes flew wide. "Yes, yes! It wasn't a dream," he exclaimed. "It all happened. It truly happened just the way we thought it did."

Lacey wanted to believe her brother, but she was confused. "What are you saying?"

"Look! Look!" Casey thrust out a finger and pointed to a spot on the model airplane between the wings.

She gazed, not seeing anything for a second, and then she saw it.

There, before her eyes, tied to a wing strut, was a tiny bottle of grape soda.

But that was not all.

Pinned on Floopy's leather helmet, lying on the workbench, was a teeny sheriff's badge.

But that's another adventure. . . .

13

A Happy Ending

A few weeks later, an answer came back from Ohio. It simply read . . .

> *Dear Mr. Nicefolk,*
> *The check for $10,000 is yours to keep.*

And it was signed *Sheriff Mugwump of Oglebee County.*

There was a P.S.: *You have a couple of great kids.*

Included was a bag of doggy bones.

Mr. and Mrs. Nicefolk were only too happy to use the money to buy an herb-packaging machine and never questioned how or why they received such a good fortune. The next harvest went so smoothly and the machine worked so handily that the Nicefolks showed a nice profit for the first time.

The extra money was used to buy the farm down the road when it went up for sale. And soon the Nicefolk herb farm was the biggest in the state.

When the next summer came, Lacey and Casey sneaked into the barn again early one morning and placed a model of a boat on the magic pad, pressed the lever on the magic box and made it big.

But that's another adventure. . . .

Author's Note

The Adventures of Vin Fiz is dedicated to the memory of Calbraith (Cal) Perry Rodgers, who made the first transcontinental flight in 1911.

Yes, there really was a *Vin Fiz*. It was built by the Wright brothers, Orville and Wilbur, in their small factory in Akron, Ohio. *Vin Fiz* had a wingspan of thirty-one feet, six inches; a length of twenty-one feet, five inches; and stood seven feet, four inches high. She weighed 903 pounds and was powered by a thirty-five-horsepower Wright vertical four-cylinder engine that could propel her up to fifty miles an hour.

Cal Rodgers learned to fly at the Wright school, soloing after only ninety minutes of instruction. At home in the air, he flew public exhibitions and received pilot's license number 49 from the Aero Club of America. In 1911, Cal entered the race to be the first to fly the United States from coast to coast, spurred on by a fifty-thousand-dollar prize put up by newspaper tycoon William Randolph Hearst that would be paid only if the flight took no more than thirty days.

Financially backed by the Armour Company, which was introducing a new grape-flavored soft drink called Vin Fiz, Rodgers began his epic flight after taking off from Sheepshead Bay, New York, on September 17, 1911. His flimsy airplane was painted bright yellow with green lettering advertising the soda pop.

Forty-nine days later, after numerous rough landings that wrecked the airplane, untold mechanical failures and bad weather, a patched-together *Vin Fiz* finally landed in Pasadena, California, the official destination for the flight. A few days later, on the way to Long Beach, where Cal wanted to land alongside the Pacific Ocean, he crashed. This time he was seriously hurt, and *Vin Fiz* was nearly destroyed.

Not one to give up, Rodgers, still walking on crutches from a broken ankle, took off again in his beloved airplane almost a month later—the *Vin Fiz* had been almost totally rebuilt. He landed to the cheers of thousands of people on a sandy beach as *Vin Fiz* rolled her wheels into the waters of the Pacific.

Tragically, during a flight in April 1912, Rodgers crashed into the surf and was killed. The exact cause was never determined. He was not flying *Vin Fiz* at the time of his death, and she survived through the years in the possession of Rodgers's mother. Little remained of the original plane that made the epic flight, and many years later, she was reconstructed and restored with parts used during the journey.

You can see *Vin Fiz* where she hangs today in the Smithsonian National Air and Space Museum.

CLIVE CUSSLER is the internationally best-selling author of the Dirk Pitt® novels for adults. He is also a true-life adventurer, having discovered more than sixty sunken ships with his crew of volunteers.

Mr. Cussler lives in Arizona.